T0358745

Into the Sea

Social Fictions Series

The titles published in this series are listed at *brill.com/soci*

Into the Sea

By

Ash Watson

BRILL

SENSE

LEIDEN | BOSTON

All chapters in this book have undergone peer review.

Library of Congress Cataloging-in-Publication Data

Names: Watson, Ash, author.
Title: Into the sea / by Ash Watson.
Description: Leiden ; Boston : Brill Sense, [2020] | Series: Social
  fictions series, 2542-8799 ; volume 34
Identifiers: LCCN 2020021984 | ISBN 9789004433830 (paperback) | ISBN
  9789004433847 (hardback) | ISBN 9789004433854 (ebook)
Classification: LCC PR9619.4.W374 I58 2020 | DDC 823/.92--dc23
LC record available at https://lccn.loc.gov/2020021984

ISSN 2542-8799
ISBN 978-90-04-43383-0 (paperback)
ISBN 978-90-04-43384-7 (hardback)
ISBN 978-90-04-43385-4 (e-book)

This book is printed on acid-free paper and produced in a sustainable manner.

ADVANCE PRAISE FOR
INTO THE SEA

"You have to be an extraordinary writer in order bring to life what is remarkable in the ordinary. In this beautifully crafted work of sociological fiction Ash Watson does just this, linking the most intimate of local details in Australian everyday life to the big issues of global history and society."
– Les Back, Goldsmiths, University of London

"A beautifully written pause-and-think novel that invites you to ponder on lives lived in and through the complexities of the present. Watson limns her characters in vivid technicolour showing how the push and pull of historical circumstances play through lives lived in seemingly ordinary registers. Will change how you think about the local and global forces that shape you."
– Nick Prior, University of Edinburgh

"An apparently simple but actually profound odyssey, not just into the heart of modern Australia, but also into the living core of what we like to call modernity."
– David Inglis, University of Helsinki

"With a whip-smart irony that is equal parts chilling and hilarious, Ash Watson has written a deeply affecting and keenly observed sociological novel set in the bubble of middling white Australia, post 9/11. We follow Taylah, a young school teacher who is unsure if she wants the glossy 'next episodes' of marriage and children but is firmly pursuing this social script nonetheless, even across the waking nightmare of the IKEA showroom. But this is a coming-of-age story that – refreshingly – never delivers us an easy ending of individual epiphany. Instead, Watson reveals the slithers of space in Taylah's everyday life and relationships where visages of consumerist distraction, social/media spectacle, lazy nationalism, and the simmering fear of terror, give way

to ennui and insights that quickly slip away again. Slicing through the moments where personal troubles and social problems collide, *Into the Sea* urges us to reflect on the ways that neoliberalism mediates our intimate lives and deflects our attention away from the things that really matter to us."
– Ashley Barnwell, University of Melbourne

"This novel brings to life everyday aspects of an 'ordinary' slice of Australian life. The sights, smells, sounds, taste and feel of the worlds experienced by the characters are artfully evoked. The patois of Australian speech, the mundane activities and rituals that structure the characters' lives, the weather, the food they eat and the homes, streets and landscapes through which they move are all detailed in language that makes you feel that you are there. Readers will be drawn into the narrative, and along the way, catch vivid glimpses into Australian culture."
– Deborah Lupton, University of New South Wales, Sydney

"This engrossing work is a powerful reflection on the lives we lead and their relationship to collective memory. It unites sociological observation and narrative form with a distinctive and exciting voice."
– Mark Carrigan, University of Cambridge

"*Into the Sea* wonderfully animates the cultural sociology of everyday life, offering as it does a deeply moving and provocative series of insights as to how seemingly ordinary human beings maintain grace under pressure as they live out their lives against the backdrop of a perfect storm continually serving up moments of risk, pleasure, challenge and uncertainty. Watson's characters and story are based in contemporary Australia, but her exquisitely honed writing depicts a compelling sociological story that can be universally appreciated."
– Andy Bennett, Griffith University

"Watson offers up a fine example of the sociological imagination creatively rendered; connecting for the reader the personal troubles of

Taylah, Caleb, Brett and co. to the public issues of our time. *Into the Sea* is a reminder that our individual experiences are part of something much bigger, that we are not simply spectators of the events – small and momentous – that punctuate everyday life. Watson's highly evocative writing quickly draws the reader into the mango memories, sunburnt childhoods and hot chook lunches of the book's characters. But underneath is always a darker undercurrent, as the characters struggle with and against the good, bad, change of neoliberal agendas and the social conditions of late modernity. A must read!"
– **Sarah Baker, Griffith University**

For my family

CONTENTS

PREFACE

Australia is many things to many people but one idea of it still reigns: Australia, the lucky country, a hot hard-but-easy place that we stop to venerate a few times a year. One of those days is New Year's Day, the day that in 1901 Australia was federated and the day this story begins with. Other days of significance mark death by war, death by crucifixion, a Queen's birthday, the Birth of the Nation, the Saviour's Resurrection, the Labouring People, the People's Show Day and a Melbourne horse race. These events fold into collective memory, mixing with the heat and the sand and the smell of rain, the roar of the crowd on grand final day, fashioning a young country and fresh way of life. This story is (mostly) set here. It's about the spaces a lot of us have grown up in – places built atop history and legend and dream and myth.

Under this southern sun anyone can have a go at life and get out what they've put in. This land is a place to stand on, to climb up from, a steady footing fair-go that makes you and will help you make your mark. Work hard, have a family, have a backyard with real grass and lie back and enjoy the freedom.

That's how the anthem goes, anyway.

ACKNOWLEDGEMENTS

First and foremost, thank you to Andy Bennett and Sarah Baker, who supervised my doctoral research project and keenly supported the creation of this novel. Thank you also to Les Back, who warmly took on the supervision of this project while I was in London. In 2017 I had the privilege of undertaking an Endeavour Research Fellowship at Goldsmiths, University of London, and am grateful for this scheme. This experience changed my life. Thank you to Patricia Leavy who continues to mentor me with enthusiasm and generosity. Thank you to all the colleagues who have supported my work. Finally, thank you to my friends and family for your patience, your care, and your love.

ACADEMIC INTRODUCTION

Into the Sea is an experiment in sociological imagination.

The story follows Taylah Brown, a white Australian woman in her mid-twenties, who teaches primary school and lives with her boyfriend Caleb in Sydney, Australia. She's busy, close with her family, has supportive friends and enough money to go on holidays and is pretty sure she does want to marry Caleb. Things seem perfect. She's living the good life. Taylah is happy – but is she fulfilled? Is this what she *wants*? Is this the shape of the life she wants, or is it just the easiest trajectory, the path of least resistance? Here these aren't just Taylah's questions – individual in scope and nature – but sociological questions.

Over the year 2014, Taylah lives through work, parties, friendships, her relationship, a funeral, a wedding, shopping, and family issues. The fictional story line of Taylah's everyday life interweaves with real national and international events and issues from the year.

This novel resulted from a project I undertook to contemporarily explore what C Wright Mills called the promise and cultural meaning of sociology. Together with ethnography and literary analysis, I used the arts-based research method of fiction writing to creatively explore the tensions in this Millsian idea. For students reading this book, this story will give you some material to think through sociological ideas and connect the dots between personal troubles and public issues.

While writing Taylah's life I was exploring the everyday processes of relation that link biographies and histories, as well as the neoliberal context within which these relations are contemporarily lived through. The individualistic common sense of the neoliberal imaginary poses a problem for public sociology, as Michael Burawoy has pointed out, considering the hostility within neoliberal regimes to the very concept of society. Trying to address this problem, my research led me to the work of Benedict Spinoza, a 17th century philosopher who sowed the seeds of contemporary affect theory. From Spinoza I drew conceptual tools for considering the meaning of how we are constituted within and by our social relations, and for thinking about individuality and agency in a located and relational way. I believe that Spinozan concepts may help enliven sociological imagination as something we *do* and can do together. To ground and realise the promise of a Spinozist sociology in this novel, I considered the temporal and spatial ways that moments and narratives are made meaningful. I focus on particular forms of Australian cultural meaning to consider the value of exploring and utilising these for affectively *thinking with* sociology. The novel braids together each of these conceptual elements, bringing them into tension and resolving them in various ways.

While this novel stands alone as a creative work, pedagogical considerations did inform its overall design. Crafted to help students traverse the (often dry) canonical themes, *Into the Sea* attempts to brings to life what it means to think sociologically. The chapters of the novel are not thematically structured, however key sociological themes do orient and drive the narrative. These include class, culture, rituals, identity, youth, gender, sexuality, family, globalisation, consumerism, terrorism, and social change. Rather than present a sociological argument about these disciplinary concepts, the narrator of Taylah's story floats critical ideas about social life which take a sociological perspective.

If there is a key point I hope readers take away from this novel and from the broader research it connects to, it is the one that I make at the end of Chapter One: we become the stories we tell. This is not a new idea but one I have worked to make sociologically significant, and significant through sociology. That we become the stories we tell rings true for the discipline and in everyday life – to paraphrase Bakhtin, meanings take shape in narratives and it is with meaning that the knots of narratives become tied and untied. This narrative considers the promise and cultural meaning of sociology. It is my hope that *Into the Sea* is a bed for sociologically-imaginative questions to flower in.

CHAPTER 1

On the first morning of the year the train takes nearly three hours to get from Sydney up to Mareebra. They pull out of the sluggish city and skirt the northern estuaries, shooting over brief, high bridges and plunging into the black mouths of mountain tunnels. Turning their heads together, the passengers watch a white seaplane hum by. It cuts down the emerald valley in a race toward the water. They pass platforms of people who, waiting for other services, picture death for a second as the train whips past, blowing plastic rubbish around their feet. Then, as they reach the outskirts of town, Taylah Brown gets mango memories. Remembering here is tasting: the sweet dark yellow of her late childhood and teenage years, in a city-town on the east coast that's close enough to the ocean for rain but near enough to the outback that flies are a permanent fixture. The green grass. Brown grass. Trampolines. Cricket wicket wheelie bins. Bats and backyard fruit trees. Suburbs designed so there's plenty of room to breathe.

Taylah, as settled as she can be with a hangover and an empty stomach on a hard-backed old seat, stares out the window at her fracturing reflection as the train cuts arcs up the Central Coast. Her boyfriend Caleb smiles at her as she daydreams, pulling his freckled arm back from around her shoulders to tuck her blonde hair behind her ear. He wonders what she's listening to. Every now and then when he gets a song they both like he shows her his screen, and Taylah smiles back. Caleb is tall and also twenty-five, with a crooked nose thanks to a high elbow he copped once in school footy. Taylah turns toward him as he pinches the top of his nose between his furrowed eyebrows. Having come prepared, she fishes around in her handbag for something that might help. Caleb yawns and accepts the paracetamol and cold water she offers. He sighs once he's washed the chalky pills down, head back and eyes closed, like they're working their magic already. Taylah drops her insulated bottle back into the bag at her feet and re-tucks her hair. Her fingers keep trailing after it stops at her collarbone. She's only had it short half a week, and isn't used to the new length yet.

They're catching the train north to stay a few nights with Taylah's folks. Caleb's only got four nights before he'll take the train back to Sydney for another year of work. Taylah has a couple of weeks left of summer holidays until she and all the other teachers start again with school. Two weeks of sunshine, swimming, and cold ham and fruit to eat. They've packed lightly for this trip. A duffel bag each – his grey, hers striped cream and blue – with swimmers, phone chargers, new books that'll be lucky to get read and just enough days' worth of cotton undies and linen outfits.

The train winds around another long corner, and an old couple walk past Taylah and Caleb to check the route information on the carriage wall. The old man, one hand perched on his wife's shoulder, traces the mapped tracks with his free fingers and they nod quietly together at the necessary knowledge. Caleb smiles at them as they make eye contact on their way back, then arches his hips skyward to free his phone from his shorts pocket again. Photos buzz in from last night. He and Taylah spent it at a small party at a friend's place, a couple they know from university who rent an apartment with a hazy, horizon view of half of the Harbour Bridge from their kitchen window, to watch the fireworks and ring in the New Year. Taylah grins as Caleb flicks open the notification. He thumbs through the selection, angling the screen towards her, pausing longer on the shots they've been tagged in. Drinking. Kissing. Lighting sparklers. Playing cards. Faces flushed and sunburnt. The girls dancing. The guys laughing with their arms around each other.

The train skirts the left bank of a wide brown river. Taylah texts her mum to let her know they're ten minutes away. The message sends and Caleb points out a fisherman reeling something in. Sunlight catches the silver tinny. The man inside arches backwards, one hand clutched to a once-red bucket hat. The train passes too quick for them to see what he's caught, pushing north-west as the river runs down and out towards the sea.

The sky opens up to them as the train pulls out of the scrub. The pre-recorded loudspeaker pronounces Mareebra wrong again (you've got to smile in the middle to get the ee's right), and when they step out onto the platform the humidity hits. Taylah's mum Liz clocks them instantly. She beeps her car horn and waves from where she's parked. They smile and set off in her direction, bags over their shoulders. Liz would normally meet them right outside the train but it feels like fifty-six degrees and, Taylah turns to tell Caleb, she's probably not got any shoes on.

Three steps down the ramp towards the four-wheel drive Caleb exhales heavily.

'Shit it's hot,' he says.

The cicadas nearly drown him out.

As kids, everyone collects the cicadas' abandoned dried brown skins off the paperbark trees and sticks them to the front of their school uniforms, like dull medals for knowing where the bugs hide and surviving the ride home on the bus. If they weren't too hot or hungry, Taylah and her older brother Brett would take their time walking home from the bus stop to find as many skins as they could. They'd fill their pockets with them, careful to not let them crush and slowly, throughout the long after-school afternoon, make them cling to the back of their mum's curly hair. One time they managed seven – or maybe nine, depending on who's telling the story – before Liz realised and chased them round the yard, threatening the wooden spoon.

On the platform the fat controller blows his whistle and the train eases itself back into the journey.

'Sorry kids,' Liz says once they're in and have kissed and warmly squeezed each other hello. 'Forgot my shoes.'

Even though it's technically the rainy season, Liz Brown has the deep tan you only get after fifty-something Australian summers. Yellow swimsuit straps glow under her floral sarong.

'Nice dress,' Taylah quips as her mum turns out of the carpark. 'New is it?'

Liz is quick back. 'Just picked it up this morning when I stopped to get you a hot chook for lunch.'

She squeezes her daughter's knee with her left hand. The dress, which Liz bought in Queensland over a decade ago, with Taylah in tow, has been to nearly every east coast beach here and as far as Thailand. The soft, light, loud fabric is a familiar feature in many of their summertime family photographs. Liz's laugh bounces through the car and out the open windows. Taylah lets her hand hang out into the breeze, only half listening as Caleb tells her mother about their Christmas with his parents in Wagga Wagga, instead watching the street.

The way home comes back to her. It's worn in. A muscle memory. Right, left, straight through the roundabout that the council's Christmas tree stands on each December. Every inch of its seven-meter height is still covered in the paper plates that local school kids paint like baubles over the last few days of school. It's a Mareebran tradition. They don't use real ones because the plastic would probably melt in the sun. Liz waves to a passing car she recognises, Jan from the council in her white sedan, and points out the residential development being built by the highway. The road into the estate is all painted and done, silver streetlights hang over the bitumen, but they haven't laid grass yet. Red-brown dust ices everything. Liz raises an eyebrow. It's owned by some Chinese company, she says, accentuating the words. She doesn't know anyone who's bought there but says the land's all been snapped up.

They turn left once they're past the petrol station, then left again, right at the traffic lights, and right into their cul-de-sac. 21 Allambie Close. Mrs Brown flicks her hand at the lack of rain as she pulls into her driveway and parks the car on the lawn, ceaselessly carrying on the conversation. Red fallen flowers from their towering Poinciana tree litter the yellowing grass. Caleb picks one up as he jumps down out of the car. A few other yards in town are coloured with trees like this. Caleb's always preferred the rough branched, soft flowering Jacarandas that explode lilac at the hot end of spring. He doesn't say that but Taylah remembers, watching him drop the flower.

A soupy breeze picks up and rolls red blooms across the driveway. Mr Brown has the garage door open. The cars are out on the lawn because the garage is half full of other people's stuff. Blue eskies, beach towels, and camp chairs all left behind after the party they threw last night. Forgotten miscellanea from the early hours of the new year. It looks like a garage sale where everything's free as long as it was yours to begin with. They know the neighbours and friends who own the all stuff will get around to collecting it eventually, when it's cooled enough to walk down the street. Taylah and Caleb get their bags from the car boot and set them down inside the living room, ready to help with the rest of the clean-up.

***

At 10:30 pm the night before, Caleb did the rounds of Steph and Michael's matchbox-sized half-of-the-bridge-view apartment with another bottle of sparkling wine. They kept the windows open and two white pedestal fans whirring on either side of the lounge room. Street noise carried up and into the windows. The closer it got to midnight the louder the party racket ballooned. Whooping, breaking glass, multitudes all laughing, bodies making their way towards the water or some house party on foot. A karaoke party a few streets away peaked hours too early. Horses clopped around with police on their backs. Ambulances cried. Champagne flutes clinked aboard the yachts. An intensity coursed through and well beyond their tiny kitchen, a blooming ecology of parties and gum trees, of kisses and taxis and cash and the feeling that this night is something special, and they were part of it. Even far from the Harbour you could feel the pressure build. Sydney, the fizzy city, with an hour and a half left to pop.

Caleb melted into the 60's style grey armchair next to Jessie and Jack on the peach toned floral lounge. The seating clashed perfectly with the blue rug, low timber coffee table and basic white Ikea bookcase being used on its side as a TV stand. Steph and Mike had found the eclectic old furniture via second hand sites when they first moved in together. Steph fawns over the strangers'-life-full stuff. Dylan laughed in the hallway behind them and Jess turned the volume up on the TV, calling out to Steph that it was on now. They had muted the show, waiting for the annual highlight reel: a video mash up of the past year put together by one of the pop news stations, played at the same time every December 31 as far back as any of them could remember. Taylah sat next to Jack on the lounge as the presenter in the middle of the news desk started an animated intro monologue. The seven of them – Caleb and Taylah, Steph and Mike, Jessie, Jack, and Dylan – gathered closer around the screen. They weren't going to see themselves in the footage, but that wasn't really the point. You spectate through the year and re-spectate on New Year's Eve.

'Well folks, it's time now to take a look back at the year that's been. Twenty-thirteen. Two Zero One Three.' He paused sincerely for the camera. 'It was the best of times, it was the worst of times.'

The other two presenters laughed right on cue. One hundred and fifty years on, Dickens is a prime-time punch line.

'No seriously folks,' the main host turned his face up to the lights again and adjusted the front of his blue product-placement suit. 'It's been a cracker of a year. It had everything and we've got it all again for you tonight. The music, events, sport, celebs, and all the sticky stuff in between.'

The female host continued on about her favourite news stories from the past twelve months, the political melodramas turned vox pop topics turned memes.

Steph perched on the arm of the lounge next to Jessie, careful to not knock down the camping mattress balanced against the wall to her right. She shook her head at the screen. 'God, I just love this thing,' she said. 'You forget what happens so quickly.'

Jessie grinned up at her, agreeing.

'Such a shame Elle is working tonight, Jess,' Steph said to her again.

'Yeah,' Jessie nodded. 'Stupid girlfriends and their stupid waitressing jobs.'

Another male presenter, slightly older and in a grey suit, jumped in laughing before throwing to another replay.

'What even did happen this year?' Caleb asked, pouring the rest of the wine into his glass and setting the empty bottle down on the floor next to his feet.

Mike leant forward, resting his beer on the back of the lounge. Steph eyed his perspiring bottle and passed him one of the stubby coolers she'd set out on the coffee table.

'Same as always, mate,' Jack said.

The female presenter read something about Red Carpet Season from the teleprompter and Jack nodded along.

'Not that that's bad,' he kept on, 'but it is always the same. A few political gaffs, a young pop star who's not even Australian being a bit risqué. The classic underdog success story to wrap it all up.'

'Same shit, different year,' Mike agreed. He ran his fingers through his swept-back fringe and pulled his beer cooler down to check how much was left in his bottle.

'Exactly,' said Jack. 'This,' he gestured towards the sports awards red carpet replay running on screen, 'is absolute rubbish.'

'Oh, puh-*lease*,' Jessie shook her head and reached for the bowl of corn chips. 'Don't act like mainstream culture is some superficial insignificance.' She grabbed a handful and continued with a mouthful of food. 'I know you watch this when it's on. But yeah, nah, man. You're so wise thinking it's bullshit. Just another sign of humanity's decline. Fashion and D-grade celebrity headlines heralding the end of the earth and us blind masses just gleefully lapping it up.'

Her tipsy sarcasm worked a treat. She grinned at the group's laughter and carried on.

'It only feels like nothing now cause you're only remembering the stories from, like, last year.'

'You are so right, babe,' Steph said. She flicked her long ponytail back over her shoulder and reached for her wine. As she drank, the saturated strawberry in the bottom of the glass slid forward with the bubbles, smacking into her top lip. She jerked her palm under her chin to catch the drips as a fireworks flashback drew their attention to the screen.

Jessie smiled as the colours cracked. 'It's better when you compare the music and clips from twenty and thirty years ago.'

'Haven't you ever looked them up?' Taylah chimed in, 'To see the difference over time.'

Jack exaggerated swivelling his head from right to left, Jessie and Steph to Taylah, and looked over to Dylan and Caleb for backup.

Mike, laughing, offered another round of beers.

***

Liz and David's old friends from Queensland, Tony and Sue, are staying down for a few nights as well. They live a day's drive north.

They own a vet clinic, have two adult kids, a cat, a cockatiel, and were married twenty-nine years this past spring. When they're hungry enough to eat, the women organise in the kitchen. Liz had bought two hot chooks and some fresh bread rolls from the little grocery store on her way to collect her daughter and Caleb from the station, so there's something easy to do for lunch.

'It's our turn for a rest,' David winks at Tony, referring to their barbecuing last night.

They stay out the back leaning on the pool fence. Starting the year the same as always. Caleb laughs lightly and stays with them, taking up David's offer of a beer from the back fridge.

A simple store-bought roast chicken for lunch is an easy ritual that, for Taylah, is knotted with the very idea of home. She can close her eyes anywhere and smell the white meat, feel the weight of her mum's white plates in her hands and hear mum's feet on the kitchen floor as she moves between the chook and the bin and the sink. Like always, Liz pulls their hot lunch from the chicken's bones and separates it onto the usual plates, keeping the stuffing to one side, humming along to the radio. Taylah gets a salad ready. She finds some lettuce, two tomatoes, a jar of marinated feta cheese and a red onion in the fridge. Laying them out on the dark bench top she takes a serrated knife from the wooden block on the counter. Liz nods towards the new place she's keeping the plastic chopping boards, moved from beside the microwave to the drawer on the left of the sink, knowing what Taylah's looking for next before she has to ask. Sue butters bread rolls, separating and taking them out of their plastic bag one at a time, and spinning the bag closed again after removing each one. Padding the hours out. As she works she updates them on her daughter, Rosie. Rosie has just turned nineteen and is busy drinking her way across South East Asia. Sue worries about her being home before March, when university starts back again, even though she promised them she would be.

'She really liked her first year, I think,' she says about Rosie's double business and journalism degree. 'She did one class on internet media stuff, advertising articles, you know. I think she did alright in that. She says she did anyway. She wrote the funniest little piece about the fascinators everyone wears to the Races.'

'I saw you shared that,' says Liz. 'Did it get enough likes?'

'Oh, I think so, I don't know. She didn't really say.' Sue pauses to wipe the sweat off her forehead with the back of her hand and sighs. 'It's nice for now and all, but I don't know if this is the kind of job she should be going for. It's fun, but there can't be real money in it, surely.'

Sue looks to Liz, questioning, and Liz can only shrug in return.

'Especially,' Sue continues, 'if she's always holidaying instead of actually getting work experience or some kind of internship. If only we knew someone. Maybe she'll transfer to teaching. I don't know. Who knows?' She slices open another roll and shrugs her shoulders, sighing. 'Not me.'

Liz offers Sue a smile and turns to her own daughter. 'Maybe you could talk to her Taylah. I think she'd like to do teaching if she's not sure about media. You should tell her about it.'

Taylah nods, knowing she won't, thinking university is the last thing on Rosie's mind. At least, that's the story her latest uploads show. She's got nothing going on online except pidgin-English jibes about motorcycles and photos of four-dollar cocktails on the beach. Taylah tells Sue she'll send Rosie a message if she wants her to, angling her eyes to the ceiling away from the half-chopped onion. When it's diced she separates it into the salad bowl, wipes her onion tears and looks in the pantry for more ingredients.

'That's just what kids do these days,' Liz adds.

Sue doesn't look convinced. She pulls her white shirt away from herself a few times, trying to circulate some air, obviously more uneasy about the whole thing than she really wants to talk about. It's the *these days* part of Liz's answer that clouds things: trying to swallow how days can feel so different here and now from how they were here and then. That relentless rolling-on.

Liz carefully separates the wishbone from the rest of the first chicken and puts it to one side. She always saves them and dries them out.

'I guess so,' Sue sighs. 'She'll figure it out soon.'

Liz puts one bag of hot juice and bones into the bin and starts on the second chicken. 'Well, someone's coming home,' she says after a moment of quiet.

'Who?' asks Taylah, confused.

'In the plane,' Liz points skyward with a piece of chicken, registering the distant rumble of an aircraft above them. 'They've probably just had their seatbelt signs turned off, if they're coming from Sydney. Can't you hear it? City living is wrecking your ears, girl.'

'There are so many planes. I must just tune it out.'

'Anyway, you two are going away soon, aren't you?' she says to Taylah, knowing full well they are, moving to change the topic.

Sue turns towards her. 'To Asia as well?'

'Nah,' Taylah says, taking a tin of corn from the pantry. 'We're going over to the U.K. at Easter, just for the school holidays.'

'Exciting. That's a long way to go.'

'Yeah, well,' she says, 'Caleb's sister is getting married. We haven't seen her in ages, but she wants us in the Bridal Party, so it's a good excuse to go. They live somewhere around London, I think.'

'I tell you what Sue,' Liz says. 'I am over fifty and I still haven't been taken to Europe.'

'Oh, you'd just love Italy,' Sue says to her, dropping the butter knife into the sink. 'The food. The shoes!'

They both laugh.

Taylah says to Sue, 'Rachel's actually marrying someone she met when she was backpacking around Vietnam, you know. And he's going to be a doctor soon so, you never know about Rosie. It might happen for her too.'

Liz lifts some dark barbecued skin from the plate and pops it in her mouth, smiling at Taylah.

Sue rolls her eyes. 'Oh yeah,' she laughs. 'I wish.' Reaching for the butter again, she says to Taylah, 'It won't be too long for you two though, surely.'

'Yeah, maybe,' Taylah replies, avoiding both Sue and her mother's eyes.

Sue looks across conspiratorially to Liz.

The trick, Taylah's already learned, is to not give anything away – not certain feelings or the hint that anything is unresolved, not plans that she's in on or accidentally stumbled upon or is trying to set up herself. You play naivety.

'Nearly done,' says Liz, making her way to the sink and then rinsing her hands of chicken bits.

While they finish preparing everything the three women settle into a comfortable silence, Sue arranging the bread rolls onto a plate, Taylah locating salad dressing in the fridge, Liz loading finished-with plates into the dishwasher and taking out clean cutlery from the drawer. The kitchen hums with potential, with the kind of happy-quiet where you can contemplate the good things to come because you're surrounded by people who make dreaming up bright things, like holidays and engagement rings, easy.

***

The replay of the fireworks from the previous New Year finished as Mike brought four more beers in from the kitchen for Jessie, himself and the boys. Taylah glanced at Caleb and he smiled back at her, skolling his last mouthful of wine and taking a cold bottle from Mike. Steph passed the bowl of chips around. The fairy lights she strung up before everyone arrived blinked yellow and green. The blue-suited host on screen told them to buckle up.

'Shush, shut up, it's on, it's starting, sit down,' Steph sang as she called them together again.

Footage focused on a red dirt landscape meeting the ocean and then dissolved into an overnight time lapse of Sydney's CBD.

'There we are,' Mike pointed to the screen, like your mum would when you were kids if Australia was ever on TV.

The shot zoomed out from the city to capture the entire hot whole of the country. Steph rested her arm around Jess's shoulders as a fireman saved a house from bushfire. The close final seconds of a yacht race ran again, and a packed stadium sang its song for a football king. A bungee jumper closed his eyes, arms out wide, and let go, face falling from fear to euphoria.

'Christ, I could not do that,' Jack said.

Before the thought could linger there was sunshine, pandas, and two newborn twins. Protest signs. Freezing people lined up in the dark outside for a shiny new tech release. The Prime Minister and the President of the United States waved to the waiting media. Another Prime Minister inspected a dry outback community and cuddled koalas and stood next to new jet planes. Hundreds of people who had made the news flicked past on screen, their lotto wins and lavish weddings and pets and competitive house renovations. The year condensed into a mass of plain faces. The video wrapped up with a running mash of positive messages that tapped into a deeper place inside you than they would on any other night. As each second played the end of the year shone brighter. Midnight was fast approaching. The footage faded. Steph sighed. They clapped and turned up the music again, muting the TV.

There was a rush of forward momentum and then, four more bottles of bubbly down, the countdown came on and they were counting backwards from ten with their arms around each other in the tiny kitchen, along with the rest of the southern states on the east coast of the country. Five. Four. Three. Two. One. Fireworks bloomed across the black sky. The bridge rained a parade of gold sparks down into the waiting Harbour. They danced and kissed and a billion people still in the year before watched the spectacular-spectacular on their own TVs. Caleb wrapped his arms around Taylah, holding her from behind, and they grinned at the high arc of the Bridge sparking in the distance, what they could see of it between the other apartment blocks and eucalyptus trees. The change was intimate: the clock face reset like it does every night yet this difference in time is heavier and more seen than any other. This glowing moment, an annual lighthouse even when you try to avoid the sharp overhype, ties people to each other. And not just this group of half-adults, in one lounge room with a floral couch in a tall apartment block by the water, in one brightly lit up city in a tiny bottom-hand corner of the globe.

'Cheers guys,' said Caleb.

'Yeah, cheers.'

'Happy New Year.'

***

Tony loads another bread roll with meat and mayo and pepper, and Liz lifts another large scoop of salad onto her plate. It's stinking hot outside, even where they decided to eat, on the back patio in the shade but, as the general rule goes, it's better to be out than in. Taylah passes the salad dressing down the table and asks for more chicken up her end. Talk turns to the end of the holidays.

'Busy year then?' Tony asks Dave as he swallows a bite of his lunch.

'Yeah mate. Too busy.' David shakes his head like he always does in January. 'Too much time in the office and not enough out on that gorgeous old river.'

Tony laughs. 'You're telling me.'

'I reckon I'm about ready for a career change.' He leans back into his chair and stretches his hands behind his head. 'Full-time fisherman.'

Liz rolls her eyes to Sue.

'If only it'd pay the bills hey,' Tony says.

'If only,' says Liz. She smiles down to the other end of the wooden table.

Their pet Labrador, Teddy, lifts his dark chin up next to her. He's snuck in from his usual afternoon napping place, under the clothesline on the grass, having smelt the chicken. He knows he's got a much better chance of convincing Liz for food than Dave. They bought him four years ago just after Taylah and Brett first moved out. They didn't plan on leaving the nest at the same time but that's the way things happened. Teddy's been their baby ever since.

'Oi,' Dave says to the dog. 'Ted. You know better than that.'

He points out to Teddy's spot at the clothesline and Teddy ducks his head under the table, pretending he didn't hear. They all laugh at him, even Dave, and Liz leans down to scratch his ears.

'I can't believe how fast he's grown,' Taylah says.

Sue laughs. 'We still say that about you.'

'Yeah,' says Liz. 'And babies grow even faster than dogs.'

'And take all your money,' Tony says, and Liz and Dave laugh.

'Christ mum, give us a couple of years.'

'Who can even afford to have kids these days,' Caleb jokes.

'Ah well, you're doing the right thing,' says Dave, lifting a pile of salad onto his plate as he talks. 'Just keep working hard, you'll be able to get yourselves settled soon enough.'

Taylah and Caleb share a look, and nod along with the well-anticipated lesson.

'But no one's gonna just give it to you,' he adds, pointing his fork in their direction. 'All this talk about housing and whatever. Things are always hard. You've got to earn it. Save your money. Not throw it away on bloody lattes and what-not. And you don't want everything in life handed to you anyway.'

'No, Dad,' Taylah agrees.

Teddy sits intently next to Liz's chair and she feeds him some chicken from her plate, patting his soft head. Dave pulls a shocked face and Teddy pads over to him, pink tongue out, tail wagging.

***

An hour past midnight Jess had the video playing again. She peered onto Steph's laptop keyboard, searching for the volume key through a haze of bubbling wine and gin. She found it and turned the volume down, then turned it up again like she meant to the first time. She called out to no one in particular for the music to be shut off. Caleb was closest to the speakers but was busy sleeping on the lounge. Mike danced in the kitchen as Jack looked in the fridge. Steph wrapped her arm around Jess's waist. The year's story played again.

***

Just before seven o'clock Liz takes the quiche out of the oven that she's reheated for dinner, a leftover that wasn't eaten last night.

'You know, I was thinking of doing something like Rosie is myself this year,' she says to Taylah and Sue, setting the hot dish down on the stove and folding the green tea-towel back over the oven rail.

'Like what?' Sue pulls six plates out of the dishwasher and sets them out along the bench.

'Asia?' Taylah asks, filling a plastic jug with water, genuinely wondering what her mother's on about.

'No, no, a degree. A class of some kind.' She smiles and shrugs her shoulders, asking them what they think. 'Business too, maybe. Maybe arts.'

Sue smiles. 'I don't know where you find the time for all these things.'

'Oh, you can do everything online now.'

'I shouldn't be surprised.'

Liz takes the pie server out of the drawer and starts lifting hot slices onto each plate. 'I thought it might be good. Something to keep the old brain ticking.'

Taylah throws the plastic wrap covering the leftover lunch salad into the bin and carries the bowl to the dining table. Caleb smiles at her from the lounge, getting up from where he's been sitting with Dave and Tony, nursing a bottle of beer and talking over the end of the news.

'Stupid bitch,' David mutters at the presenter.

'Dinner's ready,' Taylah interjects on her way back to the kitchen.

Her dad smiles up at her and the men lift themselves from the lounge. 'What's on the menu?' he stretches.

The sun burns orange as it heads for the horizon. White soap bubbles in the sink.

***

Taylah turned the music down so they could hear the man's voice on the clip, playing the video again.

'It's good,' he said. 'It's been bloody good.' It's the product-placed presenter.

Jess passed Taylah a drink that she and Steph had made. It was clear with ice and lime, and it was late and the drink too strong but Taylah downed it anyway.

'Just one more, guys,' Steph pleaded to the others not near the laptop. 'It's early.'

Jack and Dylan had no chance of finding a cab and the last train to their end of town was leaving in twenty minutes.

Jess fluffed Taylah's dyed-blonde bob as she finished her drink and told her she loved it, again.

'Just one Steph,' Jack slurred, dancing out of the kitchen. 'We've gotta go.'

***

Caleb helps Liz take the dirty plates back to the kitchen. Sue collects the salad dressing and tomato sauce. Dave has moved outside, first to feed the dog and then to chase him, and now to get the last remnants of festive rubbish from the patio. There's still the odd party popper and bottle cap in hard to reach places that need to go before Teddy decides he's hungry again. Dave wheels around the recycling bin and says to himself he'd better hose the back patio down before it gets too dark. Taylah starts taking down the Happy New Year signs.

Tony laughs and calls out to them. 'Did you get a good look at this, kids?'

He's standing in front of a huge sheet of butcher's paper that's taped up on the side of the house.

'Bloody hell,' he says. 'Don't take this down before you get a picture.'

Taylah leaves some half deflated balloons and turns around to see what Tony's talking about. He's reading a large list of New Year's resolutions they made at the party last night, near the side gate where they had people come in so they wouldn't have to traipse through the house. It's an endless messy black scrawl. *Lose weight*, one says. *Smile more*, says another. *Drink more beer*. Tony laughs at that. *Go fishing. Save money. Run a marathon.*

Dave grins. 'I bet there're some crackers on there.' He bends the hose in his hands to stop the water running. 'She'll want a photo to send to everyone.'

'Was yours fishing?' Tony calls back.

'Nah,' Dave says, leaning on the pool fence. He points to the top right corner. 'Mine's up there.'

See kids more.

Taylah smiles.

He calls out again. 'The beer one's mine too.'

Tony reckons the best one on there is *buy lotto tickets from a luckier shop*. He goes inside to find Liz and Sue. Taylah reads through the hopes, jokes and promises. She thinks the list was her mum's idea, no doubt. Liz has always been a fan of New Year's resolutions. She's the only person she knows who makes ones she can keep.

Liz, Caleb and Sue all come outside with Tony from the kitchen. They read through them, laughing, sighing, agreeing. Liz ducks back inside to grab her phone for a photo. Sue tells them hers was *travel*.

'Not that this hasn't been a very relaxing trip away from home,' she says to Caleb. 'But somewhere a bit further might be nice.' Despite how she frets over her loose-end wandering, Rosie's photos give Sue itchy feet.

We try to become new people in January. That's the psychic reorganisation the New Year brings. It feels shallow but it can run deep. If nothing else it gives us something to do, and someone to be.

Liz takes her photo and she and Sue sit at the back table again.

'That was such a fun idea,' Sue says, patting Teddy's head.

Liz agrees. 'I'll be able to remind everyone what they wrote and check how they're going in February.'

'Check how they're going next week,' Caleb jokes.

Taylah thinks of what her resolution will be as Caleb adds *save money* and *travel* to the wall.

***

Fresh drinks in hand, Dylan and Mike joined the girls to watch the video again.

Surfers. Pandas. Twins. A landslide. Famous wedding guests. A Hollywood bride. The Pope on the cover of TIME. A wide shot of Earth from space, shot with heavenly perspective. Time lapsed milky way stars from the desert. The winning goal kicked through four posts by a man wearing stripes. A small child swore and fell off her pink bike. They laughed like they did when they watched it the first time.

'So bad,' Steph wiped her eyes.

Then it jumped home to last January and the icons played. Uluru. Kangaroo. Opera House lit up in blue. Obama ended the footage, speaking over a singed koala being offered water to drink.

'Change will not come if we wait for it,' Obama told them.

Cut to a coast scene. Purple fireworks. Green.

'Change will not come if we wait for some other person or some other time.'

A recycled chorus from years ago said on some other side of the Pacific hadn't make the producers blink. The words and the fireworks fade out over a sea of people.

'We are the ones we've been waiting for. We are the change that we seek.'

Steph wiped another tear from her eye, somewhere between laughing, crying and sleep. Jack said something about what this might mean in twenty or thirty years.

Mike cradled his warm beer in both hands. 'Yeah.'

'Mediated meaning.' Jess smiled at her own insight.

But it's even closer than that. Despite the muted light, the end-of-the-party time-to-go-home haze, the screen doesn't really work to separate.

Caleb called out from the lounge, 'Change Obama is not from 2013.'

***

The paper is easy to pull down. Taylah unsticks the last bits of black tape now her mum's taken another photo with her and Caleb's resolutions on there.

'Don't think you'll get away with giving up now,' Liz jokes. 'I've got the evidence. You're the one always saying that things last forever on the internet.'

Taylah doesn't think she'll need reminding now she's inked *keep a journal* onto the list. She's given up resolutions before, the same ones it feels like, to her, that other young women write down everywhere: lose weight, learn French, lose weight. She smiles at her handwriting, wrapping up the resolution and warming herself on the mirage of the better woman she might be. Not that the journaling is for anyone to see, necessarily. It's more for thinking life through a little more just by pausing to write a bit of it down.

The little life we get stuck in, the routine of traffic and deadlines and mealtimes can make us feel like maybe we're missing something, too busy surface-level living to do anything bigger or better or real.

Taylah tucks some loose strands of short hair behind her ear and takes the paper to the bin, smiling at Teddy as she goes.

Writing things down might help her see it: we become the stories we tell.

CHAPTER 2

The following Saturday, raucous kookaburras fill the air as Taylah and her mother wake to the artificial sounds of their respective alarms. They shower, taking it in turns even in separate bathrooms so that each shower is hot and the water pressure stays strong. Once she's clean and smelling of sugary tangerine, from the shower gel her brother gave her for Christmas, Taylah plucks two stray eyebrow hairs and rubs a tanning moisturiser over her skin. With big circular motions over her arms and legs, she works quickly so the cream is dry before she starts to sweat.

Liz fries two eggs, one each, and they eat them on toast at the kitchen bench together, lightly browned multigrain seeds crunching in their teeth, margarine softening the crust, Taylah spreading more crumbs than her mother does. They both drink flat whites – the homemade version, pod-machine black coffee with microwaved skim milk poured in – and half listen to the breakfast show running on the TV in the background. There's little news this early in the year. Just cricket scores and ads for upcoming seasons of reality TV. The tennis hasn't started yet, but the season is about to so there's a segment about which sports stars have already arrived in the country. The banter between the hosts is slightly off, a half-beat out of sync with the camera crew and therefore wildly uncomfortable to Taylah and Liz – for Taylah because she never watches morning TV, and for Liz because these aren't the usual hosts.

Taylah finishes her last mouthful of egg and gives the screen her full attention for a moment. They're robots, she thinks, *nearly* perfectly lifelike robots with straight white teeth and no flyaways, soft feet so accustomed to wearing heels they mustn't sweat or ache, bodies so attuned to being Spanxed the material doesn't roll out of place or leave red marks in their skin. Probably. Taylah sits a little straighter and pulls at her waistband, shifting it slightly higher so it sits more comfortably above her hips. Liz turns to the television too, considering the on-screen faces like Taylah does, or almost like

Taylah does, thinking instead about how tired these women must be and whether they claim their Botox spending on tax under the category of workplace uniform.

Taylah's father walks into the kitchen from outside, clocks the different TV hosts, and wonders aloud where the usual two are.

'Sipping margaritas in some private tropical resort, I'd say,' Liz answers, 'being waited on hand and foot.'

'How do you know who the usual breakfast TV hosts are?' Taylah asks, thoroughly confused.

Her father shrugs. 'How don't you?'

***

Before leaving the house, mother and daughter approve each other's outfits and, after Liz changes her shoes, they drive east to the Farmer's Market. The drive takes forty minutes. They do it mostly in silence, comfortably, breaking into song when a classic comes on the radio – Phil Collins, Madonna, Savage Garden. It's a balmy 29 degrees with a slick coat of humidity and the promise of a cooling easterly breeze. Twice on the way Taylah declares the day to be perfect. Big sky, bright blue and empty of clouds. Clean, clear light.

The road there winds around small mountains, passing yellow-green fields with horses, cows and chickens. Egg farms dominate the area. As they cross the big highway the farms give way to thick rainforest, a brief strip of blackbutts and grey gums that stop abruptly, pushing against grey timber fences and the outskirts of master-planned suburban development. Taylah shows her mum a photo that her brother posted last night. Brett's sitting in a beer garden with two friends, each of them in white t-shirts, drinking golden schooners, smiling up at the camera. Taylah holds her phone steady, screen angled up towards her mum, which Liz quickly glances at after coming out of a roundabout.

'Oh good, it fits,' she says. 'I bought him that shirt.'

'It's nice,' Taylah says, liking the picture and scrolling on.

***

The Farmer's Market sprawls the concreted pathways and sports courts of a primary school. It isn't just fresh fruit and veg, which take up several large stalls at one end of the outdoor basketball court – the market is largely populated by jewellery designers, candle sellers, juicers, chilis and chutneys, sweet baked goods, fortune tellers, fresh pasta makers, leather goods, pot plants, handbags, and about half a dozen food trucks that rotate each weekend. This is what brings the people in.

Arriving, Liz lowers her car window to pay the $4 parking fee with coins that Taylah dug out from the bottom of her mother's handbag, and they find a free space not too far from the entry as someone else reverses out.

'Christ, it's so busy,' Taylah exclaims.

'Mmm, thought it would be,' says Liz. 'School holidays.'

They enter the grounds and immediately pass a French crêpe stall and a burger van. They idle past a cake stand that has three tables full of rich cream buns, red velvet cupcakes, carrot cake loaves and shortbread.

'Before Christmas was much worse, with everyone doing their present shopping,' Liz says, carefully eyeing the sweets and nodding hello at the woman selling them.

'Yeah I bet. God, these look so good.'

They smile at the cake lady who smiles back, ready to recommend a slice if either of them lingers over anything just long enough. Liz and Taylah point out various flavours to each other, like raspberry and white chocolate.

'Ooh,' says Liz.

'Yummm,' responds Taylah, dragging the word out.

Not ready to buy any cake, Liz spots a coffee van ahead and asks Taylah if she'd like one.

'Sure, I could go another. We should come back later for cake,' Taylah murmurs appreciatively, in earshot of the cake lady, smiling again at her tables. 'Take some home with us,' she adds, completely ambivalent about whether they should actually do so or not.

They walk on ahead and Taylah notes the dumpling van to her left for later.

'Dumplings,' Taylah says. 'They smell so good. I'm ready for lunch now.'

'Not yet you're not,' Liz laughs, light and sharp at once.

'I could be,' Taylah frowns, annoyed at her mother's tone because she just wanted her to agree that the dumplings smell delicious, and because she's already sweating, and the day is too hot. She thinks of all the dumplings she used to eat, well before lunch time, when it was market day at her university. A dozen or so stalls would pop up each week, capitalising on the endlessly hungry students with compulsory classes and the rolling pressures of assessment. Felafel wraps, gözleme, nasi goreng, paella. The rich smell of hot oil and sesame enticed Taylah every week one semester. One plate of six pork dumplings, loaded with soy and sweet mayonnaise, plus a diet coke and a pork bun. She smirks to herself as they take their place at the end of the coffee line. Taylah knows the exact voice and expression that her mum would have used if she'd seen her habit, eating what Liz would consider to be a full meal before also having a mid-afternoon lunch after class – though she'd be more concerned with the money waste than the multiple meals, Taylah admits to herself, carrying on the argument in her head.

'Soy milk in yours?' Liz jokes to Taylah.

Taylah pulls a face. 'God no.'

'Helen drinks it in her coffee instead of normal milk,' Liz says about one of her friends. 'I tried a sip when we were out last month. We all did, it was hilarious. I don't know how she does it.'

'Can't she drink normal milk?'

Liz shakes her head.

'Yeah, right. I'd rather drink it black, I think, if I couldn't have normal.'

'Me too. She doesn't like the taste, though.'

'Fair enough.'

Two kids dart in front of them as Taylah and Liz go to take a step forward – two boys in shorts and brightly coloured t-shirts, their flat brimmed caps almost falling off their heads as they chase each other between the adults in the coffee queue.

'Whoops,' Liz says, surprised as one boy runs into her leg. It's not a proper slam, just a rough brush past that doesn't bother him, or her really, in the slightest.

Taylah raises her eyebrows.

'Little roughians,' Liz says affectionately. 'You were so quiet at that age.'

Taylah nods, watching them run back towards their parents as their dad yells out to them. She has no idea what age they are. Three? Seven?

'All you wanted was to stand next to me, listening to the grown up conversations while your brother tore about all over the place like those two.'

Liz turns towards Taylah so she half smiles at the boys, softening the instinctive expression she was wearing so it better matches her mother's. A swift pendulum swing from bristling to bemused.

'Oh, do you have any cash?' Liz asks, patting her pockets despite only ever keeping her purse in her handbag. 'I've just remembered I forgot to get some.'

Taylah shakes her head. 'Won't need it.'

'I'll get some out after this. There's sure to be an ATM here somewhere.'

The man working the till on the coffee van finishes serving the couple in front, then smiles at Liz and Taylah so they step forward to place their order. The milk frother roars into life and Taylah repeats what they want: two skinny flat whites to take away, please. He takes her card, and she scolds herself – there was no point in saying 'to take away,' they only have take-away cups. *Idiot.* She watches the card reader as it processes the payment, relieved when it beeps positively and a green tick appears on the screen.

'Name for the order?' the man asks, holding a sharpie to a cup.

'Taylah. Thank you,' she says, and she and Liz step left into the awkward throng of people waiting for their drinks.

***

An hour later they are caffeinated and carrying new fridge magnets that look like large buttons, a citronella candle in a large blue pot, two more candles (one vanilla and one champagne scented – handy to have at home as gifts, Liz tells Taylah as she buys them), and a bottle of homemade barbecue sauce, all distributed across Taylah's handbag and a shopping bag Liz remembered to bring from home. Liz peruses a jewellery stand, moving the hanging necklaces carefully with her fingers and making small talk with the stall attendant. Taylah stands nearby under the shade of the stall awning, furiously texting Katie and Jessie.

'So what the hell are you going to do?' she asks.

Jessie doesn't immediately respond.

'Murder,' Katie jokes.

Jessie has just shared, in an angry misspelt tirade of messages, that her girlfriend has cheated, and all hell has broken loose.

Taylah sends a private message to Katie, outside their group chat with Jess, asking her what she thinks.

'I'm so not surprised,' Katie replies. 'She's always seemed so sly. And is Jess even that bothered about her?'

'She's pretty upset now,' Taylah says.

'Yeah, I guess,' Katie replies. 'They used to be so intense remember? But we haven't seen Elle round for ages now. Always "working" or whatever. Apparently.'

'I dunno,' Jessie says in the group chat. 'I don't think we can work it out. And I don't really want to. I'm too pissed off and I just know I'll think about it forever. Every time we'd get close I'd just be thinking about them together. God what a fucking chore. I'm actually shaking.'

'You can come stay with me,' Taylah replies. 'I'm up at mum's for the rest of the weekend but after that is fine. You're more than welcome.'

'Same,' says Katie. 'The couch folds out.'

'Thanks,' Jessie says.

'What do you think of this?' Liz calls to Taylah, holding up a chunky orange necklace made up of tiny beads against her neck. 'I don't have one in this colour.'

Taylah moves closer to look more carefully, running her fingers over it and considering the particular burnt shade of orange. Her phone vibrates in her hand. 'Yeah, I like it. It's really nice. How much?' she asks.

Liz flips it over and finds the little circular tag. '$29.'

'Get it, for sure,' Taylah says.

'I don't even know,' Jessie texts. 'I just can't believe she'd do this. Why would she do this?'

Taylah gets an eyeroll emoji from Katie in their separate message.

'Because she's a psycho,' Katie replies.

'At least now you know,' Taylah says. 'You had suspicions, right?'

'Well yeah,' Jessie says. 'She says they only slept together one time but I'm so sure they've been seeing each other more even if they weren't fucking.'

'What a bitch,' Katie sends. 'Where are you now?'

'Just sat outside the apartment in my car.'

'Ok come over immediately,' Katie says. 'I just got home.'

'No it's ok,' says Jessie.

'Go,' says Taylah.

'Seriously,' Katie says. 'Just come now. It's a bit early for red wine but I can google how to make Bloody Marys and I think I have some chocolate. You need to have a good bitch and a cry.'

Liz pays for the necklace and puts it in the shopping bag Taylah's carrying. 'Any updates?' she asks. Taylah had told her the basics – Elle had cheated, and Jessie had just been told. Drama.

'Nah, not really,' Taylah sighs, sliding her phone into her pocket for a moment. 'But I don't believe for a second it was with some random. Katie and I reckon they know each other, through work or something maybe, and it's been going on for a while. Anyway, as long as Jessie just leaves and doesn't go back to her now she knows.'

'Easier said than done,' Liz replies. She sighs. 'She's only young though.'

'We're the same age,' Taylah says.

'I know.'

They walk on and reach the end of the aisle, half stopping to look at the hats to their left. Liz points back the way they've just walked and Taylah nods – they paid more attention to the stalls on the right side walking down and aren't in any major rush to get back home. They dawdle past a lolly stand and a small shop selling sarongs. Liz pauses and looks at the front few on the rack. Taylah moves on to the jewellery stand next door, this one selling earrings rather than necklaces. Her phone buzzes again, and she checks the messages. Jessie has agreed to go to Katie's place, and not go upstairs to get anything so she doesn't get into a drawn-out screaming match with Elle. Jessie has also shared the name of the girl Elle slept with, which she must have gotten out of her earlier this morning or last night. Katie has found the girl on Facebook and is sending them screenshots and fiery abuse.

Taylah moves her fingers over the earring stand, listening to the young designer talk about how she makes them all herself at home with locally sourced materials and sells them at markets up and down the coast. She's younger than me, Taylah thinks. Maybe by a couple of years.

'Yeah, so, I love doing it,' the girl says as Taylah picks up a pair of studs that look like tiny, fluorescent orange slices. 'It's so rewarding to like make them all with your own hands and then see people actually wearing them, you know? It's amazing.'

'I bet,' Taylah says.

The girl grins at another woman who's approached the stall and Taylah puts the orange earrings back down.

Taylah wants to do this, or wants to do something like this. She wants to have something that is hers and she gives her time to, that takes patience and care and craftsmanship. That she can hold up in her hands when she's done. Not earrings, necessarily. But some small and charming thing that becomes what *she* does, that's not a job or a hobby but somehow more essential to her life. Something that, when the people she loves pick it up or see it in the wild, they'll think of her. She'll keep a few of them, in a box high in her wardrobe, she daydreams, looking over the rest of the earrings, that her granddaughters will go through one day when she is old and they are growing up. And they'll think of her, in awe a bit as young people can be when they realise the old weren't always old, picturing the once-young woman who made these beautiful things with her careful, decisive hands. Earrings? Ceramic plates? Photographs? Poetry? Picking up another pair of small studs she thinks, I need to find my thing.

'How much are these?' Taylah asks the girl, politely interrupting her as she explains the design process to another woman.

'The price should be on the back,' the girl replies, holding out her hand for them so she can check herself.

Taylah hands them over and the girl, finding no price sticker, checks similar styles near where they had been resting.

'I think it's $19 for these. Yeah, $19.'

'Perfect,' Taylah says, taking her purse out of her handbag to pay.

'Want them wrapped up?' the girl asks.

'Um, no thanks. I might just put them on now.'

'Easy. So on card?'

'Yes,' Taylah says, holding her debit card out towards the girl.

The girl smiles at her as the payment is processed, and tells her to have a nice day.

'You too,' Taylah says, putting the receipt in her bag with her purse and looking around for her mum. She spots her, still at the sarong stand, holding up different ones against herself in front of their thin mirror. Taylah pauses to put her new earrings in, small circular studs, half olive-green ceramic and half wood.

'Yes, they're all so beautiful. I can't decide.' Liz sees Taylah and says to the shop owner, 'Oh, here's my daughter. Maybe next time.' She smiles an apology and hangs the sarong in her hand back on the rack. 'What did you buy?' Liz asks as she walks towards her daughter.

Taylah tucks her hair behind her ears and shows the earrings off.

'Ooh, very nice. Different, aren't they.'

'Yeah, I like them,' Taylah says.

'Have you found a journal yet?' Liz asks. 'You said you were going to look for one while we were here.'

'No, I haven't seen any,' Taylah replies. 'Where did you say the stall usually was?'

'Ah, I think over back near where the candle man was? Where we got the mozzie one, not the other ones.'

Taylah motions for her mum to lead the way and Liz weaves them back through the market avenues, stopping for people turning their prams around and skirting the small crowds at popular stalls, sidestepping families stopped under shady awnings where they've happened upon a cool breeze. They pass an essential oils stand that's pumping a range of diffusers. Taylah sneezes heavily and Liz turns back to her, grinning, before they hurry on.

'Can you imagine if this was your job,' Taylah says.

'What?' Liz says, not hearing properly. She slows so that she's walking next to her daughter, not in front.

'I said, can you imagine if this was your job? Spending all weekend at markets like this?'

'Driving here from wherever you live, maybe miles away. Setting up your little tarp or gazebo in the morning, getting out your boxes of supplies and setting them all up neatly.'

'Praying that it doesn't rain.'

'Exactly.'

'You'd have to love it.'

'I imagine you would. You'd be so hot.'

'And bored,' Taylah adds.

'Maybe,' Liz agrees. 'Though you'd probably meet heaps of interesting people, and you're talking to people all day.'

'Yeah, kind of. We don't really talk though, to the people selling stuff. You either ask questions about things or just pay for something or hope they don't want to talk to you.'

'Hah,' Liz says. 'For you young people, maybe. The stallholders all talk to each other. They've probably known each other for years.'

'God, that's a thought,' Taylah says. She shifts the image of her imagined future handiwork, thinking the online route is the way to go. Maybe just some of those special markets that are on around Christmas – though they're probably quite hard to get into, as a designer. She'd make the right things though, things people would want to buy, and take home and wrap carefully and watch the people they've bought them for open them before celebratory lunches or between celebratory drinks.

Maybe she could paint things, Taylah thinks, as Liz points out the stand selling journals and other stationery items up ahead. Not paintings on big canvases like actual artists paint – though maybe she could get into that if she bought a kit and took a class or, more realistically, watched some videos on YouTube. Hers would be more like those nice signs people hang in their hallways or living rooms. Old wooden pallets sanded smooth and painted white or light blue. Only roughly painted though, not totally covering the soft brown of the wood so it looks more rustic, authentic. And she could learn some calligraphy and inscribe them with modern takes on classic homely sayings: take inspiration from everywhere; you are exactly where you're meant to be; the best moments in life involve dancing, laughing and drinking wine. Something like that. They can be so clichéd, she thinks, but she'd have time to get it right. They pause at a juice stand blending fresh fruit and vegetables with ice, and Taylah shakes her head when Liz asks if she wants one. Liz orders one for herself, fishing for the right coins from the bottom of her handbag. Taylah waits to the side and sees herself as she would be: holding a paintbrush, hair half tied up in a messy bun, serene, wearing loose overalls and maybe a white t-shirt, Caleb smiling and trying to wipe off some small smudge of white – no, blue – paint she's accidentally got on her cheek. A cool breeze comes through the big open windows of the room in their house they've cleared for her to paint in, they are laughing together and kiss while she holds her wet paintbrush aloft, his firm hand pressed to her small waist, and she updates her Etsy page, spends Saturday mornings buying new paints from the paint shop, and stands alone before her wooden pallet canvas, quietly contemplating the right background tone, working into the evening with bare feet.

'Ahh,' Liz sighs, noisily thankful for the first mouth of cool sweetness of the drink.

The spell of Taylah's painting career is momentarily over. She tries a sip of the juice at her mum's insistence, asks her if there's ginger in it (there is), and they move onward toward the stationery.

As they reach the stand, Taylah's phone buzzes with messages from Katie. Jessie is at hers, she says, and is an absolute wreck but they are walking to the shop for supplies – Tim Tams, full-sugar coke and salt and vinegar chips – and will just chill out all afternoon. Taylah promises to come over once she's back in the city.

'Sleepover one night,' Katie tells her. 'We'll do a proper slumber party. That will cheer her up.'

'Invite Steph?' Taylah replies.

'Maybe. Bed space though. You can easily crash on the fold out with Jess but with more it'd be a squeeze.'

'Yeah nah fair enough,' Taylah replies, as her mum holds up a handmade birthday card and asks her if she likes it.

'Oh, cute, I do,' Taylah says. 'Sorry, getting Jessie updates. Planning a sleepover next week.'

'A girly sleepover, that will be nice. At your house?' Liz asks, rifling through the box of other cards.

'Nah, Katie's. She's in the inner west.'

'Ah yes, you said. I remember now,' Liz replies, looking through the box of cards.

'These are nice,' Taylah says to her mother and to the girl standing behind the display table, picking up a notebook with a tree fern design and instantly envying the girl's brunette curls. Taylah opens the cover, to check if the inside pages are a decent quality. The girl slides her phone into the back pocket of her jeans and watches Taylah flip through the pages.

They're simple notebooks bought from a standard stationery shop that the girl has made new covers for. Most have soft covers, but some are sturdier. She's covered the cheaper ones in printed paper. The more expensive hardback options have flashier materials – a soft faux leopard fur, one with a shell somehow glued onto the front that closes with a braided leather wrap-around string, a glittery one that leaves faint traces of multicoloured sparkles on Taylah's hands. Taylah touches most of them, not moving too quickly, implying with this exact pace that she's seriously considering buying one – that, at this point, it's a matter not of *if* but *which one* – so the shop attendant moves with her, not hovering over Taylah's every move and definitely not offering too much conversation, but just being near enough that when Taylah holds one purposefully and makes eye contact she's already reaching for the card machine.

'I'll go with this one, please,' Taylah smiles, holding out a hard-covered notebook. It has a dark purple cover, more maroon than pink – wine coloured, Taylah decides. They pages are soft, almost cream in colour, and lined with faint grey lines. The girl running the shop smiles, takes it from her and places it gently into a brown paper bag, which she closes with a circle sticker of her shop logo. Taylah watches her fingers seamlessly go through the motions, well-practiced at where to fold the bag and where to first place the sticker.

'I love that,' Liz says, having watched the shop girl bag it up. 'But not the one I thought you'd go for, actually.'

'Really?' Taylah says, handing over her debit card to the girl and picking up one of her business cards from a neat pile at the front of the table. 'Which one did you think?'

'Hmmm,' Liz sounds. She peruses the notebooks more critically. Her hand hovers over the glittery one before decisively pointing to a smaller notebook, a delicate light blue. On closer inspection the cover is a photograph print of an almost cloudless sky. Shades of blue meeting blue, slight traces of white.

'I do like that,' Taylah says.

'It's one of my favourites,' the girl says, handing Taylah back her card and her paper bag. 'A picture of possibility. But the purple is really nice too.'

Taylah smiles and notices the earrings the girl is wearing – tiny plastic bunches of grapes, dangling from each ear.

'I love your earrings,' Taylah says. 'Are they from...' She gestures towards the earring stand across the market.

'No,' the girl smiles and shakes her head, making her curls bounce. 'Can't remember where these are from actually.' She reaches up to gently touch the bunch on her right ear. 'I've had them for ages.' The six – seven? Taylah isn't sure – purple spheres swing and Taylah thinks about the orange slice earrings she didn't buy.

'Sorry,' the girl offers.

'Oh no, it's fine,' Taylah waves her hand.

'They are very cute,' Liz chimes in.

'I like your earrings too,' the girl says.

Taylah thanks her again and she and her mum head off towards the food. Taylah places her purse and the wrapped notebook into her handbag, rearranging the lip balm and water bottle and tampons and candles she's also carrying.

On the way to the food truck section they stop twice, to taste some honey roasted macadamias and for Taylah to buy a bottle of homemade tomato sauce. Passing a palm reader's tent Taylah jokingly dares her mother to go in. They both vow that they're all shopped out, and as they round a corner the dumpling stall comes into view. Liz rubs her palms together and nudges her daughter.

'Jokes on you mum, I smelled them six steps ago,' Taylah says, nudging her mother back.

They join the end of the queue and Liz peers around the couple in front to try and see the menu.

'Pork and chive, prawn and pork, chicken, or vegetable,' Taylah reads aloud.

Liz suggests they go for the share plate option of four pork, four chicken, and four vegetable dumplings. Taylah adds a can of Coke and four spring rolls – Liz is fine with her water she's brought – and they find a semi-shady spot perched on a retaining wall under the branches of a gum tree. Taylah holds the disposable plate as Liz cracks her wooden chopsticks apart before returning the favour. Her phone hasn't buzzed but Taylah checks it anyway, clicking into her messages to double check when there's no notifications on her home screen. Liz takes a photo of their lunch, getting it now before they eat too much, and uploads it to Facebook, tagging Taylah and the markets in the picture. Caleb likes the post immediately. Other likes roll in as they work their way through the plate. Taylah dunks a spring roll into the accompanying small tub of sweet chilli sauce and carefully races it into her mouth to avoid getting orange drips on her shirt.

'Ooh, careful,' Liz says, reaching for a spring roll herself.

'Mum,' Taylah begins, after sitting in silence a while, pausing to finish her mouthful. 'What do you think I should do with my life?'

Liz laughs. 'Whatever you want.'

'No, but, seriously.'

'Go to the moon.'

Liz and Taylah reach for the same pork dumpling. Realising, they grin and both recede, both apologise, point their disposable chopsticks at each other and tell the other to have it. Liz holds firm. She picks up a chicken one instead.

'Fine,' Taylah says as the takes the contested morsel. 'If I have to.'

'Why are you asking?'

'Why not?'

Liz shrugs. 'Don't you want to teach?'

'Nah, I do,' Taylah clarifies. She cups a hand under her chin as she nearly drops some of what she's eating, and reaches for one of the serviettes Liz picked up. 'I love teaching. I mean, not having a permanent job yet absolutely sucks balls. But I mean what *else*.'

Liz shrugs again. 'Travel. See the world. Have kids.'

'Yeah,' Taylah says, resigned, the conversation not quite going the way she'd like.

'That'll keep you busy. Pass the time.'

'Until death.'

'Exactly,' Liz laughs.

'What did you want to do when you were my age?' Taylah asks, watching a small girl stop to pat dog that's also resting with its owners in the shade close to them. The dog is small, smaller than the toddler, covered with long brown hair that skims the ground. It's panting, sweltering, tired, pink tongue out as the girl repeatedly pats its head.

'I don't remember,' Liz responds.

'You must,' Taylah says.

Liz considers it. 'Read all the great books. Go to Europe.'

'Cure cancer? Save the world?'

'Nurture the great minds of the next generation,' Liz teases.

Taylah rolls her eyes.

'You'll figure it all out as you go.'

'Blind, aimlessly, directionless,' Taylah jokes, monotone.

The little girl's mother finally convinces her to move on from the dog by hyping the market stalls and sweet treats to come. She gives the pup once last kiss on the head and waves goodbye as she's walked away.

Liz looks at her watch and says she can't possibly eat any more, so Taylah should finish the plate off.

'Are you sure?' Taylah asks.

Liz nods and Taylah devours the remaining two dumpling and lone spring roll, covering them in what's left of the sauce. She wipes her mouth with the napkin and takes their rubbish to the bin. Liz takes a sip of Taylah's drink and hands her the can when she walks back.

'Finished?' Liz asks.

Taylah looks around. 'Yeah, I think so.'

Liz nods and they head for the carpark.

The car is stinking hot inside so they blast the air-conditioning on max and are careful not to touch the metal of the seatbelts to their skin. Taylah sighs and unbuttons her jeans. Liz changes the radio station to find some good music and reverses out of park.

***

Later, Taylah retires to her refurbished teenage bedroom for an afternoon nap, and videocalls Caleb before she falls asleep. While she's yawning, he answers.

'Nice face,' Caleb jokes.

'Shut up,' Taylah retorts playfully.

'How were the markets? Lunch looked good.'

'Yeah pretty good thanks,' Taylah says, rearranging her grip on the phone. 'Bought some good stuff.'

'Oh god. Here we go.'

Taylah mimics him and makes a face. 'None for you then.' She reaches for her handbag that's at the end of the bed. 'I bought a nice tomato sauce,' she says, holding it up to the camera.

'Yum,'

'And a barbecue sauce,'

'Yum. Same shop?'

'No, different shops.'

'What else?'

'This candle – it's in the kitchen, I'll show you later – a citronella one for us in this nice little blue plot, it's like kind of wide, not very tall, but it's still pretty big. $20.'

Caleb nods.

'$25 actually, I think. Anyway, and I bought this notebook that I haven't actually opened again yet.' She rests the phone against the pillow so Caleb can see her unstick the sticker on the brown paper bag and pull out the wine-covered journal.

'Nice. What's that for?' Caleb asks, innocently enough.

'It's a journal,' Taylah says.

'Right,' Caleb responds.

'So it's for journaling.'

'Right. Okay,' Caleb nods again. 'How much was that?'

'Oh I can't remember,' Taylah says, putting the journal down and lying on her back on the pillows again, holding the phone up at a good angle over her face. '$15? I'd have to check. It's not like it broke the bank.'

'No, it's fine, I was just asking,' Caleb says.

'Okay. Oh and also these earrings,' Taylah tucks her hair behind her left ear and holds the screen over it. 'Can you see?' she asks.

'I can. Very nice. I like those. Is that wood or does it just look like it?'

'Nah it is actually wood, they're really nice actually. I love them. The girl had so many nice ones but I thought these were different.'

'A good outing then,' Caleb says.

'Exactly.'

They look at each other for a long moment and Taylah crinkles her nose.

'So, what have you been doing today?' Taylah asks, swapping her phone to her other hand and touching a pimple on her chin she's seen on the video.

'Nothing really,' Caleb shakes his head. 'Went for a quick run this morning because I woke up early. Probably the beers last night. I don't feel hungover though so thought I'd make the most of the morning.' He pats his flat stomach.

'That's good of you. I've just eaten all day and will continue to do so.'

'Oh well,' Caleb says. 'You can work it off. When you're back here and in your normal routine, you know? It'll fall off.'

'I know,' Taylah sighs. 'So how was last night?'

'Yeah, good. The boys are good. Dave was telling us about this horrific date he went on, so awkward.' Caleb laughs to himself, remembering.

'Hah, thought you meant my dad for a second then.'

'Nah, Dave from work.'

'I know.'

'God, I am so glad I don't have to go through that ever again, you know? The dating world has changed, and it seems horrific.'

'Tell me about it,' Taylah says. *Don't count your chickens, Caleb*, she thinks. She goes to make a joke about him not putting a ring on it yet but stops herself, and pushes the thought from her mind.

Simply via the passing of time, they've recently moved into a phase where Taylah feels awkward joking about weddings now – something light and hilarious to do when it's definitely too early for them as a couple, in the early period when people would think they're rushing it, but now it's been a few years and they actually *could* get engaged and Taylah doesn't want to seem like she's pushing. They'll start talking about it this year, she thinks.

'What are you thinking about?' Caleb asks, after they sit in silence for a while.

'Nothing,' Taylah says.

Caleb waits, wondering what nothing is and thinking maybe it is just nothing and he's being paranoid. It's just that they're on the phone, he decides. In person it would feel different. He walks into the kitchen in their apartment for some water.

'So, what happened on the date?' Taylah asks.

'Do you want me to tell you?'

'Whatever,' Taylah responds, biting her fingernail.

'Whatever?' Caleb asks.

'Sure,' Taylah says, making eye contact.

Caleb pauses, not really wanting to relay the story now, sighs and decides he wants to move past the tension more. He details the awkwardness of his friends' date, the stunted conversation and missed jokes, kissing her ear instead of her cheek, the struggle of the shift to in-person conversation when you've been talking online for so long.

'How long have they been talking for?' Taylah asks.

'Actually, only a couple of weeks, I think. But, you know, intensely. He's basically obsessed with this girl and then she's totally different in real life.'

'Devo,' Taylah says.

'Exactly,' says Caleb. 'Anyway, they go back to her house and he recognises the girl's roommate but isn't sure from where and then the next day realises he used to talk to this other girl too but basically ghosted her and now he doesn't know what to do, he doesn't even want to message the girl back.'

'And they slept together?'

'Yeah, well, I don't think they actually had sex, just other stuff you know because she didn't want to, so, but still.'

'Yeah, still. Did you tell him to stop being such a pussy?' Taylah says as she checks her eyebrows in her reflected image.

'Hah, basically. There are also plenty more fish out there though, you know? So, if it doesn't work straight away like why waste your time.'

'I guess,' Taylah says, biting her nail again.

'What are you doing this afternoon?' Caleb asks.

Taylah yawns. 'Going to have a nap now, and maybe play Monopoly or something later with mum.'

'Cool.'

'What about you?'

'Jack's coming over to play Xbox.'

'Fun,' Taylah says. There's a long pause. 'Well,' she continues, 'I'm going to sleep.'

'Alright,' Caleb says. He gazes into the camera. 'I love you.'

'Love you too, babe.'

'Talk to you soon.'

'I'll text you later.'

'Alright. Good. Sleep well. Bye.'

'Thanks. Bye.

CHAPTER 3

When you grow up here, this coastline works its way into you until it is you and you are it and the long stretch of sand is home. The Browns moved house just once when Taylah and Brett were kids. They stayed on the east coast but went south, Bonnigong to Mareebra, three hundred kilometres closer to Sydney. David had to move for work. Brett remembers their blue station wagon chock-full of cardboard boxes, their sad-looking house left behind, the endless drive. He didn't want to go. Taylah didn't want to go. Liz didn't really want to go either. All three were leaving for the first time. Their Dad said, for the umpteenth time as they pulled onto the quick moving highway, that they could have moved much further – across the vast red middle nothing to the west coast, where the sun was shining all day on big money mines before lowering itself into the ocean. The consolation prize was that they didn't. They stayed east.

Brett remembers Mareebra as a cricket pitch and Bonnigong as the blowhole near the sea. For Taylah, Mareebra is the river and mangoes and Bonnigong is the orange tree. The orange tree on their old street where the school bus would wait each morning, idling until they burst out the front door. The bus in the morning at the orange tree. The bus in the afternoon at the orange tree. The orange sticky-juicy sweet.

***

Now it's a stifling Thursday evening in February and they're getting on a tiny plane back to Bonnigong together. The sun went down an hour ago but the air seems to have missed the memo. It's hot and muggy outside. They're weighed down as they wheel their suitcases through Departures, like stones fill their pockets and bricks line their bags and each step forward is more of a struggle. It might have felt like they were all going home-home again, their first home, Dave and Liz and Taylah and Brett. But it doesn't.

41

The automatic silver doors let them inside. Crisp air-conditioning and a wall of terminal noise hits. Couples, families, and singles in suits shuffle across the polished floor one slow step at a time, anxious and excited or late. Two flights are delayed; two cities flash a loud red on the schedule screen, but the Browns' short flight north from Sydney is green. Brett sighs, almost wishing it wasn't. Anything to put off the cold, wet, coming future for a few more hours.

The queue starts way before the retractable barrier maze but Liz knows the lady who works the check-in counter – an old friend, who she called while they were in the car on the way – so they're escorted straight to the front. Nobody complains because no-one argues with a whole family, especially one that looks like this, with grief so heavy they have their own airline attendant to help carry them onto the flight.

***

Let me set the scene: the call came on Sunday at lunchtime. Taylah was home at her mum and dad's and Brett had driven up from Newcastle for the weekend too. A sudden electronic trill interrupted a family argument about the ham in the fridge and who'd go to the store for fresh bread. No one ever normally answers the landline but Liz saw the name on Caller ID: The Masons. She shushed them before answering. The Masons are their old neighbours from their old house in Bonnigong. Mr Mason would always put their bins out for them when they went on holiday. They rarely ring now with good news. Liz put her hand over her mouth as she answered and turned her face towards the kitchen window, anticipating the worst about an elderly friend. Someone the Masons played bowls with or had round for Sunday roast. Someone they'd been visiting in hospital since the end presented itself. It's been fifteen years since the Browns left, and the Masons are now in their old-old age so calls like this are more regular. Liz likes that they still call.

She inhaled sharply, lowering her head into her free hand. It was unexpected news. 'Oh God,' she said into the phone.

Her hand moved between her mouth and her forehead, clammy and lost.

'Oh God. Christ. Oh no.'

Breath caught in her throat. More words tried to get out. David and Brett and Taylah all froze, mid ham argument, Brett with his mouth open and David holding open the door to the fridge. The air soured around them and grew still. Liz started to cry – a flood of tears.

'Shit,' she said. 'What…?'

Brett was closest to her. He reached out and held his mum's shoulder. Liz nodded and swallowed and mouthed it to them.

'Sam O'Connor.'

She grabbed Brett's hand. David closed the fridge and rested his fists on the bench. Taylah swallowed. A salty burn stuck at the back of her throat. A sticky sour tart. Not orange juicy sweet. Liz didn't ask any more questions so that meant it was something bad. A sudden, bad thing.

'Thanks for calling,' she managed. 'Yeah, yeah I will.'

She hung up the phone and shook her head and that was the end of it.

Sam is a boy who lived on the same street as the Browns when Taylah and Brett were growing up – was a boy, who lived on the same street as them when they were growing up in Bonnigong.

The grief came thick and fast, like a summer storm.

Sam was ten months older than Taylah and a year younger than Brett. Sam's folks babysat them when the Browns went out, and Liz and David returned the favour. They spent Saturdays together in the pool and Sundays together at the beach. To Taylah and Brett, Sam's mum was Auntie Shirl and his dad was Uncle Mick. They caught the school bus every morning and afternoon for close to seven years, from the orange tree to school and back again, before David's work shifted them down the state. The O'Connors hadn't moved from Bonnigong. Not Shirl or Mick or Sam.

As his death came to light, people talked about Sam as being stuck in the seaside rut that sweeps up young people when they don't leave at the 'right time' and go on to bigger things. A hidden rip you can get caught in.

Liz lifted her head to relay the details and cement the fact of it. David booked them all flights for later that week. Brett called his boss to take the end of the week off and Taylah did the same, then texted Caleb about it too. Liz called Shirl and they barely spoke, but both cried for a long time, and Liz told her they'd be up soon.

Shirl had found Sam in the downstairs bathroom last night, the one they'd been forever renovating, when she and Mick got home from the surf club. Sam hadn't wanted to go. He said he didn't feel like going out to eat. They hadn't even been gone long. Two hours, not quite three. Mick had to cut down the rope.

***

When they're on board the plane they spread across two rows. Liz's friend made sure they were seated at the back because that's where it's the most empty, and they'd have room to just be. David passes Taylah his hanky and a pen across the empty seat between them. She balls the cotton cloth up in her fist, staring ahead at the sick bag in the back of the seat.

Taylah pulls her journal out of the handbag. The last page she wrote is neat and ordered. A list down the left-hand side. For the past two weeks she's been trying different ways of doing it – recounting her days, rough scribbling the weather, pensive paragraphs of feeling, trying to find a cadence for it all. Lists were the easiest. The cleanest. A simple refrain to maintain for the year: What's good? What's bad? What can change? What she can change, if everything clicks into place. She writes the date in the top right corner, *February 27 2014*, and an airhostess strides past clicking her thumb four times on a silver tally counter. Taylah looks out the window into the night. Red lights blink beside them, burning against the grey runway. The red changes to green. They hear the seatbelt spiel and when the plane takes off Taylah writes *Good:* on the page.

They're flying toward a funeral where almost everyone who'll be there is older than the reason they've come. Nothing is right about it. There's nothing good to say. This absence is bigger and whiter and sharper and even harder to deal with than death usually is. Taylah leaves the first list blank because all she's got are *Bad's* and *Change*: that black dog, the boy, the rope, the gravity. The frantic, sluggish fever that burns hot-cold enough to hang a twenty-seven-year-old lonely orange tree boy in his parents' spare bathroom at night.

***

At midday on Friday they meet Mick and Shirl for lunch at Flinders, the café in town next to Lifeline. Liz used to bring Taylah and Brett here after school sometimes for strawberry milkshakes. She thought they should go somewhere to eat because Mick and Shirl probably aren't remembering to. Well-worn routines fall away easier than you'd think.

Mick and Shirl are like you'd expect: slow moving and grey faced, shoulders sagged under their kid's weight. Carrying a grief there aren't words for. If Shirl didn't have red hair that helps you spot her a mile away, she'd blend right into the overcast sky. They pull two tables together outside under the café awning. Liz goes in and grabs a wet rag to wipe down the sticky metal top, and David takes his shoe off to wedge under the short table leg. He tests it a few times, wobbling the table tops with his palms until he gets the angle right. They order an assortment off the lunch menu. Shirley and Mick both get fish. They half talk about little things. Work, holidays, work. No one's mentioned doctors or even loneliness, not anything going wrong. These troubles are too raw, too soon, too private. The food is quick to come out and every now and then Shirl rests her knife and fork.

'Nice fish,' Liz says like she didn't know it would be, like she hasn't had it a hundred times before.

'Yes,' Shirl manages. 'It always is.'

***

When they've finished their food, without having to talk about it, Brett and Taylah excuse themselves from the table. They walk past Lifeline, the cheap second-hand store, and head down Main Street. It's an aptly named and never changing strip of old milk bar cafés with plastic white tables and those freezing metal seats. Fresh made sandwiches, fresh baked sweets, fresh caught prawns and the best meat pies you'll ever eat. Sun bleached paint crumbles off nearly every outdoor sign. The occasional one is new, outside the Greek restaurant and the women's fashion store, but mostly no one fixes them or seems to mind. It does give the place a character that the newer, slick sea towns haven't yet grown in to.

Brett laughs as they pass the video rental store. 'Must be the last one left in the country.'

Main Street leads directly downhill to Main Beach. You can smell the salt all through town but now they can taste it too.

'Remember that,' says Brett.

Sydney isn't inland but they grew up in the water, the two of them – the three of them – and the concentration of cement in the city strips the strength out. The soft, sticky, stuck in your hair crunch at the end of every sunny day. Childhood for Taylah is a yellowing film reel of bike rides, the splash her dad made when bomb diving in the deep end of the pool, and hot scones with thick lashings of butter. And oranges. And the sea. They keep on, passing another few shop fronts and nodding hi to familiar looking strangers, until the café strip ends on their side and the path opens up to the church. Prime real estate if there ever was. The funeral will be held here. The cemetery is spread across the lawn out the back. Taylah's grateful they can't really see it from the street. Neither of them can think of anything to say so they just look up towards the doorway. The roof peaks into the grey sky, leaning slightly downhill towards the ocean. The wooden front doors are closed but they'd be unlocked. A noticeboard to the left, just inside the gate, is covered in homemade flyers for piano lessons and surf lessons and a missing orange cat.

They leave the Church and pass by other old familiars on their way to the water. The park, the police station, the seafood restaurant with the brilliant view all the way up the coast. They reach the bend on their side. Main Street curls around to the right, skirting the rocks and heading south. Taylah and Brett cross to where the footpath widens around one of the town's war memorials. Taylah stops to touch the stranger's names on the sandstone, a childhood habit. The voice of her grandmother echoes in her head, telling her that, for most of them, these markings are the last sign that these men were once alive – proof that they really lived. Kicking, breathing, drinking, singing, feeling angry and happy and lost, at some point loving or nursing the idea of love. Someone watching them take their first breath. Maybe alone for their last. War memories like this dot the whole coast of the country. Names known and unknown. Brett continues on to the beach. Plastic poppies left over from Remembrance Day lodge between cracks in the stone, forming part of the landscape, working their way in where the wind can't find them.

***

Brett is knee deep in the water on the right side of the red and yellow flags. Taylah watches him, his hands on his head looking out to sea. He's still and the waves crash against him. His shoes and white shirt lay in a pile on the sand where he pulled and kicked them off, barely taking the time to stop. He's heeded their mum's old advice: you never regret a swim. He drops his head backwards, turning his closed eyes to the grey sky. His hands fall by his side. After a while he looks around the water, surveying the incoming set of waves, and dives forward into the sea before the first wave breaks. He stays underwater until he feels the second wave pass overhead, holding his breath until it burns. He exhales the stale air when he can't keep it in any longer. The bubbles force their way up. He lifts his feet off the sandy floor and lets his chest burn a moment longer. Then he pulls himself upwards, oaring his hands through the water until his forehead breaks the surface and air rushes his lungs. Taylah nods to herself and keeps walking. Another wave comes quickly and Brett dives under again, not as deep this time, letting the pull of the wave drag him along and turn him over. Water pushes past him above. He lets his knees buckle and the waves take him, carrying him passively backwards towards the beach. No boundary between him and the ocean. Affectively part of the sea. He thunders his breath out into the whitewash until it's all gone and the emptiness, the collapse and tight pressure in his chest comes again. Traces of Sam float into his mind. Images of him, them together, tanned and sandy skinned, at this beach. Brett swims and lets go in the water. Under and over. Breathing in and out. Pulled here and pushed there. Swell in the ears. Salt splashing his face. The waves. Throat burning. Chest tight. And the pain gets carried away.

***

Taylah makes her way across the beach towards the headland. She takes her shoes off and stays high on the rocks, climbing past the signs to please not go near the old (and *mostly* untouched, she tells herself) shell midden site further down where the brown rocks colour white. She climbs closer to the blowhole. There is a proper path to get there, winding down towards it from the road up top, that was worn in long before the Gong was a destination. Before the pub was built, before the clergy came and the trees were chopped down, before white sails first spilled blood into the harbour. Each step worn in over time. Footprints now buried under concrete. But climbing up from the sand is the way Taylah's always gone and so that's the way she does it. She climbs until she finds a natural seat in the rock. Close enough to hear but not get wet from the rolling suck and spew of surf. The water draws back into itself, down and away from the rock, before pushing back through the blowhole and dancing up into the air. Again. And again. A cyclical give and take of tide. Taylah takes her notebook out of her handbag. The rhythm persuades her to write. She turns past the half-finished list she started on the plane and writes,

> *Good:*
> *Bad:*
> *Change:*

The blowhole blows again and people on the path 'ooh' and 'aah' to each other.

Sam has died and she's back in a town that will always feel like home, and nothing here is different but everything has changed. The surf spews back up through the blowhole. People sing, 'ooh,' 'aah.' She writes under *Bad:*

Sam is gone.

This much is obvious. He's gone. He's gone and he's not coming back, and it still feels like he's only gone for a little while and has to come back eventually, like a sock that ended up in the wrong wash and is in someone else's bedroom. She knows he won't. He is gone and it's terrifying and ruining and sudden and sad, and she's furious and feels too much of everything. At the same time, she feels nothing at all. She'd do anything to take it back. She wants to scream and fight and run and drown and go back three days, twelve months, fifteen years and shake him and hold him until he knows they would all catch him any time he falls – every time. And this is the worst part of it. It's not about falling at all.

***

They take the hire car from the hotel on the road overlooking the coast to get to the Church instead of cutting through town. The ocean has always brought them what they need right now: that sense of something more which a lot of people get from looking up into the stars or praying.

Shirl asked them all to not wear black today, like they always do when the person was too young or too young at heart. Taylah wears white. She thinks no other shade feels right. David still wears his black suit but pairs it with a white shirt and a yellow tie. Liz is in a blue dress with her hair pulled back, and Brett wears cream chinos with a blue collared shirt. They each bring sunglasses, ready to wear them inside. The sun burns through the windows but it's freezing in the car. Taylah gets goose bumps. She runs her fingers over them, and her fingertips start to feel numb. She feels numb. This is the worst day.

Driving along the top edge of the headland Taylah realises they never made it to a hospital. There was no preparation. Nothing medical. There weren't weeks of waiting, no great reveal in a bleached room or talk about scan results and tests. The blue gown and rubber gloves are a black cloak and scythe we now expect. They didn't get to slowly consider the cause for this end of life, just acknowledge the sudden sharp fact of it. Brett holds Taylah's hand. She puts down her window and looks out to sea. None of them have spoken yet. At this point there isn't much left to say. Liz told them last night what Shirl had said: the funeral director was smart, solemn and efficient. Not a grief counsellor but a businessman, guiding the decision making for them slowly, like an oven baking bread. There were so many things to manage, Liz said. The Church. The Priest. The music, the casket, gravestone, catering, flowers. They drive past the blowhole and the ooh-ers and aah-ers, past the windswept poppies at the war memorial. David parks the car on the street. Taylah winds her window up again and before they properly stop they can already see the flowers. David locks the car behind them and passes Taylah a hanky. They move inside together and are swallowed by the crowd. Flowers line everything – the door, the pews, the altar. Picked yesterday and starting to brown.

***

The sorrow in Church feels panicked. Father Peter, the Priest, reads through the rituals and they, the congregation, fan their faces with freshly photocopied prayer books.

He reads, 'Thomas said to him, Lord, we don't know where you are going, so how can we know the way? Jesus answered, I am the way and the truth and the life. No one comes to the Father except through me.'

The Priest's words show on the projector screen behind the altar as he reads them. When he's finished the passage he pauses. The words fade into a photograph of Sam. A new song starts. Sam's mate Dylan reads a verse from a song with Mick's hand on his shoulder while Shirl holds him from the other side. Shirl cries and Mick cries. When Dylan has finished reading he rests a surfboard against the end of Sam's coffin and collapses back into the front row of the audience. The Priest takes his place again and raises his arms up to them as he talks about Church People. How mourning is not just about feeling grief, but is a process we must share and come together in through the ceremonials of religious tradition. Taylah unfolds the hanky her dad gave her and wipes her face. The song and slideshow change again into a picture of Jesus and a prayer. Sam's death tangles with the Church. Father Peter tells them about the many rooms in God's house and how Jesus carries Sam to his kingdom of heaven. Taylah wonders if Sam's life flashed before his eyes as he tied and re-tied the rope. Whether he heard the harps and angels sing instead of the ambulance siren they wanted him to survive. Whether Sam believed in all this, or if they're burying him in the wrong ritual.

At the Priest's signal, David, Mick, Dylan, and three other tall men move towards the casket. The Priest has finished speaking and it's time for Sam to leave. Everyone stands. Music plays. New photographs show on the screen. Sam as a boy. Sam running. Sam playing. Sam swimming at the beach. They cry hard and loudly, collectively. The men carry Sam through the crowd, across the right arm of the transept and outside into the sun. Shirley follows them. Liz holds her. Brett carries the surfboard. Sam waves from the projector screen. Waves crash below them on the beach.

***

On Sunday afternoon Mick and Shirl have people around for tea. Mick's brother's family come, and both lots of next door neighbours. The afternoon unfolds like almost every other one Taylah and Brett have spent in the O'Connor's backyard. Except for Sam's heavy, blinding absence. People scatter around the back patio on outdoor chairs and their eskies. Liz brought a fruit bun she picked up at the old bakery, the one with the pink coconut icing, and there are biscuits and crackers and cubes of cheddar cheese. A family from down the road turns up with oranges from the orange tree. Shirl's in the kitchen making a salad. Mick will peel prawns and cook a BBQ later. Right now he's busy showing off his collection of stubby coolers. There's the green bikini one from Cairns. The elephant one from Dubbo Zoo. Dave's using the classic Bondi Beach scene. Mick makes them pick a new cooler for each can of beer. Taylah opts for a glass of white wine with ice, like the rest of the women. It's so hot the ice hardly makes a difference. The humidity has thickened real early. A big storm is coming. When it storms here in summer the air gets so heavy you can almost see it. You feel it press into your skin right until the rain starts to fall, and someone cries *the rains are 'ere*. And the heavier the rain falls the lighter everyone feels. When the storm moves on there's a brief, light respite. And then the humidity crawls back under your skin like it never left, not really, like it was simply in the next room waiting out the rain.

They all feel strange being in Sam's house without him. He still lived with his folks, like most people his age do here for longer now, and Taylah keeps expecting him to walk outside and join the group. For the front door to slam and his surfboard to be propped up against the hallway wall. For Shirley to call out and tell him, again, for the thousandth time, to take his wetsuit off before he comes inside. There are traces of him everywhere. The basketball hoop above the garage. His dormant Facebook page. One thing we don't think of when we buy or make things is that they might outlive us.

Busy distracting themselves from the Sam-shaped hole in the universe, no one really notices Taylah move inside. She treads quietly from the lounge to the staircase. Mick and Shirl haven't touched his room yet. They probably won't for ages.

It's dark upstairs. The storm is close. Sam's room is third on the left. His window looks straight out to the water. Aside from a few downhill rows of houses and tops of gum trees, the view is all sky and sea. She can see the orange tree down the road, like the one the school bus picked them up from and they picked afternoon tea off in when they were in season. For the first time she wonders who planted the trees.

The storm rolls in like always, dragging a constant rumbling thunder. The clouds come black and green. The sun hasn't set behind the height of the houses so light still strikes the beach. The long strip of sand shines white-gold. Gulls dive for fish.

Sam's bed is unmade, top sheet kicked to the bottom of the mattress. Blue curtains open. A pile of dirty washing on the floor. Taylah wants to go through everything – remember him, hold on to him. Let him go through his things. But there's a deeper sense of privacy in the stillness. She sits on his bed in the quiet. When the thunder gets close and loud enough she feels it in her chest Taylah takes the cue to leave.

She pockets one of Sam's leather braided bracelets from his bedside table and heads back down to the kitchen.

Everyone has moved inside. Wind whips through the palm trees that guard the back edge of the pool. Rain belts down, roaring on the roof. Shirley, hesitating for half a second, runs back outside to pull the washing off the line. The clothes are already soaked and before she gets halfway out she is too. The wind pulls at her hair and the hem of her yellow dress, spinning the Hills Hoist round when she isn't steadying it. Mick chases her out, shouting over the wind for her to leave it, telling her it's too late. The rain falls harder and he bellows for her to stop.

'Stop Shirley. It's done. You can't.'

She keeps going. Mick shakes his head and runs out from under the patio to help her and bring her back. Before he reaches the line he looks as if he's been swimming. No one can hear them over the rain but Shirl doesn't stop so, shaking his head, Mick gives her a hand. They heap soaked washing into their soaked arms, leaving the pegs on the line or throwing them down onto the grass. Lightning cracks across the sky. Everyone, Taylah and Brett and their mum and dad and the other O'Connors and neighbours watch from the kitchen in silence. Wet socks, shirts, and knickers are pulled from the line. Pegs collect at their feet.

Liz holds one arm across her body and her free hand to her mouth. 'They're mad,' she says.

The line is almost empty. Mick runs back towards the house with a mountain of wet washing in his arms. Lighting cracks. And Mick trips. He yelps as he falls. Shirley turns round towards him. He's jumped at the lightning and slipped on the wet grass. The washing flies up into the air and, like a slow motion film scene, falls down again to earth. Blue shirts and brown shorts all splash into puddles of mud. Mick reaches out his hand trying to save something, anything. He goes for the catch of the century.

Time seems to freeze. There's the rest of them, inside and speechless, and there's Shirley with her wet arms full on the lawn. And there's Mick, six beers deep, on his back in the rain, muddied and soaked though. He holds Shirley's old purple sports bra up to the sky like he's just won the Test Match final for Australia. Shirl stands frozen. Mick turns his head towards her. He gives the bra one more upwards thrust for good measure. Shirley cracks a smile. She laughs. She drops the clothes on the soaking ground and laughs. Mick pulls himself to his feet and, still clutching tight to her bra, moves towards her. They hug and kiss and laugh and cry in their backyard in the rain.

CHAPTER 4

Each weekday morning at quarter past six, when the magpies start, their alarm rings. Taylah is the first out of bed. She opens the grey curtain on her side to let the light in – she read in a magazine once that getting natural light when you first wake makes you less drowsy during the day. Caleb stays under the covers with the white sheet pulled almost over his head, scrolling through his newsfeed, until Taylah's about to be done in the shower. Then he's up to turn on the coffee machine. Taylah glides out of the bathroom in a cloud of steam, hair wet and wrapped in a towel or dry and tied on the top of her head, and Caleb goes straight in. He streams a morning playlist with his phone turned against the tiled wall and drags the floor mat back from in front of the mirror to the shower door with his feet. Pyjamas pile on the floor. The plastic yellow sand-timer from the cyclic drought years, that you're supposed to suction to your wet tiles and time a four minute shower with, is long forgotten in the back of the cupboard.

Taylah's underwear is folded in the top left drawer of their dresser: black, white, nude, blue, floral, striped. Caleb's stuff is in the drawer on the right. She pulls on a pair and finds her black bra from yesterday, hanging on the lip of the laundry basket. The toilet flushes. Their neighbour's new baby cries. It's been a good kid so far, sleeping until six-thirty rather than screaming for a feed at two and four like the other bub downstairs did. Taylah's thankful she doesn't have a newborn of her own to look after, and immediately feels guilty at the thought. After trying on a knee-length denim skirt and lemon yellow sweater, and black pants with the same sweater then a light blue button-down shirt, Taylah keeps the top and settles into navy dress pants that hug her hips. Caleb turns the shower off. The coffee machine light goes green. Across the hallway the elevator dings. They have twenty-three minutes to miss the worst of the traffic and not be late for the train. Taylah punches a pod of coffee into the machine. Her mug fills. Caleb makes his own cup, still wearing his towel, and an alarm in their kitchen-side neighbours' rings. Caleb rough measures milk and oats into a clean bowl he takes from the dishwasher. The elevator dings. Taylah spoons a thick glob of yoghurt onto her muesli. Caleb's oats bubble in the microwave. He keeps his finger on the machine's stop button, ready to kill it before the milky froth overflows. Taylah spoons apricots out of a tin. The neighbours switch on their TV. Caleb squeezes out the last of the honey. Through the wall they hear the newsreader.

Anti-government protests planned.

A heat wave.

Still no sign of the missing plane.

Taylah and Caleb share a Look, pausing over their breakfast for half a moment. Disbelief gets deeper the longer there's no sign of the aircraft – how can such a big thing go off radar? It's hard to imagine there's any centimetre of Earth not being recorded by the satellites circling in space. We're so used to being constantly seen. The newsreader explains the current theory: MH370 switched off, lulled its passengers to sleep with a lack of oxygen, and auto-piloted down south. The newsreader emphasises this southern turn. This means it came towards Them – towards Us – perhaps far off the distant west coast but no one else is out there so they're running with it like the country's now connected in this. Connected in what exactly isn't so clear. Connected in feeling maybe, in disbelief and denial and fear and hope. Solemn grey-faced politicians make statements promising to find it, promising as if the plane will be intact and not a wreck.

When news about the missing plane plays people look to the sky. The news stories circle like it's still in the air. And in a way, in your mind, it kind of is – flying just out of radar sight, above the clouds and surely, eventually, coming back down into view. A continuing planeload of potential energy until there's definitive proof of its grounding.

The news cuts to the entertainment presenter for a review of a new superhero film. The city stops holding its breath.

**

Each day they do this hurried dance. Separate and together. The luckiest of the lucky country with their curtains, coffee, shower steam, bowls, and cereal boxes. More coffee, more apricots, the honey and milk. Babies getting a feed. The alarms and elevator dings. The neighbours' TV. The fridge door opening in between. The whole city pulsing through its before-work breakfast routine.

The rest of the morning goes like this: Caleb reads the news off his phone. Taylah looks at her own, seeing mostly the same things he does as she scrolls the updated happenings of mates and ex-partners and celebrities and politics and internet friends. Maybe she stands to rewrap the wet towel on her head, if it's a washing-hair day, then leaves her bowl, mug and knife in the sink and blow dries her hair in the bathroom. Caleb finishes his breakfast, rinses both of the bowls and finds a shirt, a tie, pulls his socks on sitting on the end of the bed. The elevator dings again and the school kids from apartment 303 race down the hallway to catch it. Taylah brushes her teeth and makes the bed then Caleb brushes his teeth while Taylah applies her weekday makeup. A perfume. A lipstick. She adds coloured earrings or a necklace and pulls some work-appropriate sandals onto her feet. Caleb ties his laces in the lounge room. Caleb has a six minute walk to the station and seventeen minutes on the train. Taylah's school is a thirty-five minute drive away. Taylah almost always waves at Caleb from her car as she buzzes out of the driveway.

***

Perfect white cotton clouds make shapes above the school. A single plane cuts through them overhead. An absolving breeze blows inland from the back of the ocean, carrying the kids into the iron green school gates either from the bus stop or the parent drop-off zone, where a steady stream of four wheel drives ruins the flow of traffic. The breeze dances with the kids' cotton elastic-waisted shorts, hair ribbons, and maroon KHSPS embroidered bucket hats. Karalla Heights State Primary School has sat on top of its rolling hill since 1936. The car park and computers and a few classrooms are new, but the rest of the school is the same series of stand-alone red brick buildings connected by concrete paths, half-shaded by palm trees.

Taylah is Miss Brown here. She's taught Grade Five for the past six weeks and will keep her class until June or, if she's lucky, through December. There doesn't seem to be much more than luck in it – another network of who and not what you know, unless what you know is where to be and you're fine with spinning the situation as 'flexibility.' Last year she had Grade Two for the last half of the year on the same kind of contract, filling gaps from maternity leave.

***

When morning tea ends, the bell rings out across the grounds and a drove of kids rush back to class, sweating and shiny red cheeked. The school oval where most students spend break times playing football or netball or something in between looks west over the suburbs. It cops full sun so the class sunscreen supply is used without protest. By half-past ten each of Miss Brown's thirty-two students have scrambled into their classroom, one of the demountables that were a temporary installation three years ago. A freckled, curly-haired boy finds a grass stain on his sleeve. He spits into his right palm and rubs at it, dulling the colour and soaking his white uniform. The girl sitting next to him giggles and her friend, behind them, pretends to be sick. The boy frowns at his still-green shirt and starts to suck on the sleeve instead. Miss Brown turns the ceiling fans back on and sticks her head out the door, checking for stragglers. A tall boy asks if he can go to the toilet.

'It's Miss Brown, not Mrs,' Taylah reminds him, whipping from the light-hearted laughter of morning tea to frustration, and says if he really needs to go he'd better hurry up.

The rest carry on like galahs. Chatting, turning, laughing, yelling, running down the aisles between their seats. A girl with her hair in two braids throws a scrunched up ball of paper high across the room to a boy on the other side. He reaches for it from the floor where it's landed without getting up from his seat, looking to Miss Brown to see if she's seen. She has. He pockets it. Another boy runs back out to his school bag, skidding to a stop before the door to check if he can, returning with a half empty water bottle. He skols almost all that's left as he takes it to water bottle city: the laminate bench top on the left side where their bottles live like skyscrapers, in electric colours and plastic heights. It's so the condensation is kept in one area. The other boy runs back in from the toilet and Miss Brown settles the class down from the front. It's time for History.

History is covered between morning tea and lunch each Thursday in practically every year five class across the country. Monday is reading and science and maths; Wednesday is science and maths and music and reading. Friday is sport, maths, spelling; English is every day before morning tea. Miss Brown writes *The Colonies* across the whiteboard and the kids take their notebooks out of their desks. The back wall is plastered in the cheery multicolour posters designated for the unit. British names, brown maps. Blue flags. Governors. Pictures of wooden sailing ships, iron shackles, women carrying parasols, brown and green lands cleared for crops and sheep. Stockmen. Stations. Campfires and spears.

'Today we're looking at life on the land,' Miss Brown says with a seriousness that quietens the class, just as her Mrs Fish said in 1998 and Mrs Fish's Miss Middle said in 1963.

Thirty-two blue lined notebooks fill with the same leaden things for the following forty-five minutes. Droughts and floods and bushfires, the extraordinary God-given ingenuities of tough hardy rough ready migrant battlers, the back-ache of work on un-British Crown land. The years between the First Fleet and the First World War bleed together into a thick rush of sheep, gold, guns, hangings, horses, bushrangers, boomerangs, and steam trains. When Miss Brown clicks onto the last projected photograph, she checks the time and the schedule. Spot on. She finds the related quiz as the class finish their notes, and passes the pages out – take one pass it on, take one pass it on, take one pass it on. The lesson continues as prescribed. A girl in the third row gets the highest score and wins another golden sticker next to her name on the poster on the wall. History is folded up once more. It's time will come again next week.

***

In two weeks, Miss Brown's class, along with the two other grade five classes, have an excursion to an old Farmhouse – a colonial property on the outskirts of the city that's been meticulously preserved as a living museum after winning preservation funding. Staff dress in bonnets and keep chickens. The property spreads over a large hill, like white butter on a stack of pancakes, looking down towards the Harbour in the distance. Before buildings started going up as well as out they probably watched their own ships sailing in. The kids yell about how fun life then would have been. Teachers stand together on the grass and take stabs at the value of the land.

***

On Tuesday nights Taylah talks with her mother while they both cook dinner. They video call. Separate screens set up in their two kitchens. Tonight Caleb has to work late so it's just Taylah's mum and her. David is in his office at home finishing off what he didn't get to during the day. It's always been this way, with him having more work to do than there are office hours to do it. At home it's mostly answering emails and calling people back. He paces around the little room when he's on the phone, making the grey carpet lay lighter as he walks towards the doorway and darker as he makes his way back. He sighs when he sits at the desk. He'll usually have a beer before dinner. Two if it's hot, three if it has been 'one of those days.' Liz darts in and out of Taylah's video frame, blonde curls pulled back into a low ponytail and loose strands constantly being re-tucked behind her ears. She's preparing steak, spinach, and sweet potato for her and Dave. This has always worked this way too: Liz in the kitchen on weeknights, the news or a game show playing loud in the lounge room, talking to herself and the TV.

Taylah washes and peels her own potatoes while the stove behind her heats up. She'll boil them and steam broccoli while the chicken legs roast in the oven. Liz finds some oil for the electric grill and turns it on at the wall. She cooks steak inside in the kitchen where she can keep an eye on everything at once – Dave would do it outside on the barbecue. Teddy jumps up against the kitchen windowsill, knowing it's almost dinner time. David feeds him just before they have dinner too so he doesn't claw at the door. Liz turns her screen around so Taylah can say hi to the dog, and asks what time Caleb's getting home.

'Soon,' Taylah stresses. 'He just has a meeting.'

Liz tells her that's alright from off screen, that the overtime hours will make a big difference in the long run. She's looking for the tongs.

'He's usually home not long after me.'

Taylah takes a knife from the drawer and chops the two potatoes into small chunks. She half fills a silver saucepan with water and adds the potatoes, putting the pot on the stove to boil. Liz reaches across the screen and Taylah adds a dash of salt to the pot.

'I'll just grab another pot for the greens.'

Liz always narrates the process whether there's anyone listening or not. She holds her hand over the electric grill, testing to see if it's hot yet. It won't be. She'll wait for the sweet potato to boil and drain it, get the margarine out for the mash (just a little, to soften the texture rather than for taste) before she puts the steak on. She always does. Teddy jumps up on the other windowsill to see what's going on. Liz pulls a face at him through the glass. Taylah slices her broccoli into smaller pieces. Little green bite-sized trees. When she was young her mum would ask her to check the stalks for little birds before they threw them over the water. One day, she thinks, she'll occupy her own kids with the same things. Taylah takes the top of her double boiler out and steams the broccoli over the potatoes. Her dad swears in the background and she asks her mum how he's been.

'Oh you know,' Liz waves her hand. 'Same old.'

Mr Brown is an ad man. He doesn't make the ads but organises them, or something – that's as much as Taylah knows and as detailed as she ever needs to articulate. He complains about how busy it makes him but, really, he loves it. He swears out of habit more than anything, like the pacing and the sigh when he sits.

***

61

Taylah's food doesn't need her for a few minutes so she sits and asks her mum what she's been reading. It's always something new and something good. Mrs Brown is a librarian. Taylah's taken to buying books even though when their rental lease runs out it'll be a pain to move them, and she and Caleb will argue more about the heavy, dusty, once-read books than the best way to disassemble their flat packs. Liz prefers to borrow them. They read better, she says. And she like that she's sharing the story.

'Oh, you'll love this one. Just finished it last night.'

She leaves the screen and wanders down to her bedroom to find it.

'It's a thriller,' she calls out loud enough for Taylah to hear.

Taylah's phone, charging on the bench beside her, lights up with a message from Caleb. No words, just a sleeping face and a grin. She smiles too and sends back a house and crying cat.

'Here we are,' Liz holds the book up in front of the screen, too close for Taylah to make out anything except half a knife and the colour red.

'Back it up, ma. Who's it by?'

'Oops, sorry,' Liz laughs and holds the book further away from the camera. 'S J Knight. The Bone Collector. It's a bit like all the others really, but it's got a great twist about halfway through.'

'Alright, don't give it all away. What's the back say? Worth buying?'

'It's worth a trip to the library.'

Taylah's water starts steaming in clouds so she hops up to check on the broccoli.

'Ready?' Liz asks Taylah, waiting to read out the blurb.

'Yeah, go. Still here.'

Liz clears her throat and lowers her voice like the trailers for all the films. 'P.I. Jenny Winter has put away more criminals than all her ex-work mates at the Hope Island Police Department combined, but when a cold case from ten years ago is suddenly re-opened, she finds herself at the centre of the investigation – on the other side of the police line. Who is The Bone Collector? Can Winter prove her innocence? When all the signs point the same way you'll ask yourself, did she do it?'

'Woo hoo,' Taylah says, blowing on a piece of broccoli she's fished out with a fork. 'Lady P.I. on the wrong side of the law. Maybe I will have to find myself a copy.'

'It's a good one,' Liz says. 'Right, better do the sweet po-taties.'

Taylah moves the broccoli off the hotplate, but keeps the lid on to keep her greens warm for the next six and a half minutes. Liz does the same with her sweet potato mash and turns the gas on under her greens. Liz's veggies and meat will be ready at exactly the same time. Taylah's still getting her timing right. Everything with practice. David walks into frame on Taylah's screen and leans his face down close to the camera.

'Hiya Tay,' he grins, and stands back to swig from his beer bottle. 'Glass of wine, love?' he asks both of them.

Liz shakes her head no and Taylah takes a glass from the cupboard behind her.

'Don't mind if I do.'

'Smells great. What are we having?'

'Chicken,' Liz says as Dave inspects the two pieces of steak.

'Dee-licious. Can I help?' he asks.

All that's left to do is eat.

Taylah pours a half glass of wine for herself from a nearly empty bottle in the fridge. Her phone buzzes on the bench with another emoji from Caleb. A bike and an OK sign. He's on his way.

'So, how's work?' David asks Taylah, taking a sip from his wine.

'Yeah pretty good. Good class really,' she says. 'Still strange only talking to children all day. I feel like I'm forgetting how to have an adult conversation.'

'Ah well, you're doing alright so far.'

Taylah laughs.

'You'll be off soon anyway. All organised, is it?' he asks.

'Yeah, nah. Pretty much I guess. The flights have been for ages, so, and not too much accommodation to worry about. We booked the train tickets from London this past weekend so now just deciding what to do when we get there.'

'Good,' her dad says. 'You'll be fine,' he adds, reassuring himself more than anyone, the big white missing plane circling his mind.

There's a pause until Liz asks, 'Are you going to see a show?' from off screen, setting out two white plates on the bench.

'Hopefully,' Taylah says. 'There's stuff on every night in West End. We might wait until we get there, Loz from work reckons they do cheap tickets outside the theatres, so we'll probably just wing it.'

The oven beeps and her chicken is ready. Taylah turns it off and takes the tray out with an oven glove on her right hand, the purple one her Nan bought her when she first moved out. Her brother Brett got the same in blue. She plates up the chicken and broccoli for herself and for Caleb, wrapping both plates in foil and leaving them in the oven until he gets home – in about twenty minutes, she guesses with a glance at the clock.

'Okay, dinner's up,' Liz announces.

Dave gets two pairs of cutlery out from the drawer and carries Liz's iPad over to the dinner table. Taylah sets up cutlery at her bench. Liz follows David into the dining room with their plates.

***

Taylah carries her journal around everywhere in her handbag but doesn't know what's good or bad or can change about her everyday things like this. She follows her usual orbits between work and Caleb and friends and, on some weekends, the actual city. There's not much give between the pull of these private magnets.

She tries writing about what's on the news but it's depressing and often there's nothing good, only ever some beauty-pageant 'world peace' change. In her own life there's lots of good – all the usual things are, good and easy, so much so you never stop to really think – but then there's only personal bad and such small-scale change: a full-time contract, being more fit, owning their own place, walking 10 000 steps a day, the right diamond ring and knowing when it'll come but having a pre-perfected surprised face. A mountain of things to become a better individual, better than before, things that photograph well and keep the momentum of her life rolling towards the next chapter, any new chapter, a step up in the story she's living. Because if it slows at all, if the next part of the plot is hard to make out, the routes you run each day between your usual things start to burn something in your brain. And whenever you're not distracted enough by whatever is meant to be coming next you can only feel a heat, an impatience, a frustration.

And then something like Sam happens, and you're trapped between the lines on the page. The good bad change lists won't translate.

***

The last day of term is a Friday. Normally Term 1 ends on Holy Thursday, and Friday they'd get off, even at the State Schools, starting the Easter holidays with a good Good Friday joke and with chocolate eggs hidden in the shade outside the classroom. This year the kids get their school treats and hat parades two weeks early because the holy holidays have fallen at the start of Term 2. Luckily for Taylah and Caleb the year has worked in their favour. Taylah will get seventeen mandatory days off without needing to take sick leave – just enough time to make return flights to the U.K. worth the expense.

When it's time, the kids sprint into the still, hot afternoon air of Friday freedom, promising to ask permission for sleepovers and bike riding adventures as they climb into their parents' cars. Soon after, the teachers lock their classrooms and shake off any lingering responsibility over left behind hats and forgotten water bottles. Everything can wait until next term. More pressing matters are at hand – the office staff organise an afternoon tea on the last day of each term: tea, coffee, cold beer, white wine, ham and chicken sandwiches, sugar biscuits, crumbling pastries, sliced fruits, mini quiches and curry puffs, and always a chocolate mud cake from the grocery store that one of the office ladies picks up at lunch. Someone's also brought hot cross buns this time, considering it's Easter, some of the new kind packed with sticky date and butterscotch. The staffroom television plays the afternoon news on mute in the background above the fridge which the three male teachers have gathered around, magnets to the beer inside. Mrs Williams, one of the Prep teachers, swallows her mouthful of chicken sandwich and points up at the screen.

'Just awful isn't it. Bloody terrifying.' Footage of the still-missing plane and a muted crowd of crying relatives transitions to a family photograph cropped around a laughing fifteen year old blonde girl, missing since last weekend from a northern suburbs beach. Her photo has played three times a day since the news first came in. 'God I hope they find her soon.'

Taylah shakes her head and finds a napkin to wipe her sticky hot cross bun fingers on. She's followed the story, less out of persistent interest than inescapability, and the police appear to have some leads but are still pleading for public assistance. 'She could be anywhere.'

'She'll be out west, the cops know that.' Morgan, their new twenty-four year old sports teacher chimes in beside them. 'Of course they've taken her west. They always do. That's why we haven't seen them raiding any homes along the shore,' she says. 'No point.'

'Mmm,' Mrs Williams bobs her head and finishes her sandwich.

Mr Hutchins, Year Four, says that's why he and the wife agreed to let their ten year old get a mobile phone. 'Just in case, you know. Better safe than sorry. There're a lot of sickos out there.'

'That's what I think,' says Mrs Williams.

'Have they found her mobile?' Taylah asks.

'Haven't found a thing,' Morgan says. 'Just a burnt out car up the highway that may or may not be connected.'

'No witnesses or anything. How awful,' Mrs Williams says again, picking up her cup of white tea from the table beside her. 'What is going on with the world.'

'Broad daylight too,' Mr Hutchins says.

'Everyone there probably didn't even realise what they were seeing,' says Morgan. 'Pretty young girl gets into a car. They do that every day.'

'I hope I'd realise, if I was there when something like that was happening,' Mrs Williams says.

The newsreader frowns at the camera, pausing for half a second as the segment ends before smiling into a story about a polar bear born in a zoo. The footage focuses on the sleeping cub, then pans out to the throngs of crowds and cameras behind the fence line, all pointing and flashing and recording the moment from every possible angle. Taylah smiles and moves to the bench to pour herself a cup of coffee.

'Not long now, hey,' Lauren says as she weighs up having peppermint or green tea. 'When do you leave again?'

'Tomorrow night,' Taylah says. 'It's come so quick.'

'The past few weeks have flown, haven't they? It'll be Christmas again before we know it.' She laughs and opens the green tea sachet. 'You'll have such an amazing time. London is just the best fun.'

Taylah says she can't wait. They both rest their backs against the kitchenette bench, looking across the room and blowing into their respective white cups to cool down their drinks. The staffroom is bulging with noise. The staff laugh together, hovering around the back-board of photos or the fridge, or grouped in the middle of the room where the food is, sharing photos from their phones and telling each other their plans for the holidays. Nearly everyone with young kids is going camping somewhere along the east coast, as is the Easter tradition.

Mr Sander, the Principal, laughs in the middle of the room and helps himself to a biscuit and a mini meat pie. He holds them in a white napkin and calls for everyone's attention, wanting to say a few words for the end of term.

'Thanks everyone, thanks.'

The conversations die out and the staff all angle themselves towards him, shifting in their seats or moving sideways so they can see.

'I just want to say a few brief words, and then you can all get back to your nibblies.'

Mr Grange, one of the PE teachers hovering by the fridge, passes Sander a beer.

'Cheers mate,' he says and turns back to the room. 'We've had a great first term this year. Ten weeks have absolutely flown by and, even though it still feels like summer, Easter is here and every single one of you deserve a very restful break – even if your kids think otherwise.'

Everyone laughs about the heat and nod their heads at their inexhaustible children.

'Like I said this morning at assembly, school holidays are just as much for mum and dad as they are for kids. If not more so,' he laughs. The room laughs again with him. 'So now, a quick toast.' He raises his beer bottle to the room and everyone raises their bottles and teacups and biscuits. 'Here's to a great start to the year. May your campgrounds be sunny, your glass always full, and your children late sleepers for the next fortnight. Cheers!'

Everyone calls cheers together, raising their drinks and snacks higher before taking another sip or bite. Sander shakes hands with the people nearest to him. Lauren, still beside Taylah, finishes her tea and places her cup back behind her on the bench.

'Well, that's enough for me,' she says. 'I'm off.'

Taylah puts her half-empty cup down to give Lauren a hug goodbye.

'Enjoy your break,' Taylah says.

'I will,' says Lauren. 'And you have a safe flight. Thank Christ you're not flying to Asia.' Lauren laughs, not even half joking, like the destination was what went wrong with the plane.

CHAPTER 5

Taylah has never found it easy to sleep on planes – not that she's been many places far enough away to need to. Her hips get numb and her feet itch and she stirs each time they change the lights. She'd probably find it easier if they did the whole seventeen thousand kilometres in one go, or in a higher class, but with the rest of the 99% (of international fliers) they sit in rows of ten and switch planes in Singapore first, and then Dubai, before making it to London.

***

Their first day they walk a fifteen kilometre loop from the Zoo over the river and almost back again, catching the tube home after just making it for an hour in The National Gallery before closing time. That night they compare their blisters, eat at the closet pizza chain, and go early to bed. Before all of that, before their aching bodies remind them they are a body, in the morning there's sunshine and midday brings the rain. It's a light rain, a sprinkling you can hardly see that joins with exhaust fumes and somehow soaks everything right through. Caleb laughs when he notices Taylah's jeans. On the front the denim is dark and wet from walking around in the weather but the back of her legs are still dry. Taylah pronounces the river out loud a few times to get it sitting right in her mouth.

'Tems. Tems. Th-aims. Tems.'

Caleb stops to take a snap of the river and Taylah puts the umbrella down while he takes the picture, holding both arms out to the side and smiling like there isn't any rain. Caleb laughs. The skyline behind them is as perfect as the postcards. The old stone Tower still standing along the riverbank. The soaring skyscrapers. The Gherkin. It's strange being in a city you've seen so many times before on screen, like you've walked it all before. Like a game. Like a dream. It's a different kind of place to the fixed Londons past – not the wooden, single-bridged and stone-walled Saxon city nor the private-gardened nucleus of the great Empire. A postmodern transformation past the terror and tragedy and supposed romance of wartime Britain. Despite the global economic down-turn it's a skyline of cranes. A not quite (or not yet again) coherent place. Maybe it always feels like this in real life as we read places through their written histories. Taylah puts the umbrella back up after Caleb takes a wide panorama and they turn away from the river, in search of a repeatedly recommended Australian coffee shop.

***

By the time they reach the Eye the rain has eased off a bit. It falls even lighter than before. Not that anything feels less wet.

'Shall we?' Caleb asks, pointing up to the slow turning trip.

'I think we have to,' Taylah tells him. 'We wouldn't leave Paris without climbing the Eiffel Tower.'

A man standing under the awning at the front tells them it's a two-hour wait.

'Bugger,' Taylah says.

'Come back?' Caleb offers. He takes a shot of the white steel from underneath. 'We've got a couple of days before Tippley. Early tomorrow morning might work.'

'Deal,' she says. 'The weather might be better.'

The man under the awning behind them laughs. 'Don't count on it, sweetheart.'

'Yeah, sweetheart,' Caleb teases in a put-on accent once they're out of earshot. He reaches for Taylah's hand and they head up the stairs to the next bridge.

***

The next morning the weather is fine again and they catch the tube to the south side, starting with The Shard and planning to try the Eye after. Paying the ticket price, they line up for the 70-odd storey elevator ride with the other tourists who could afford it. At the top, on the upmost level where the spiking glass opens up to the clear heavens, Caleb and Taylah look quietly down to the river. They tower over Tower Bridge, a feat of modernity itself only a hundred years ago, a tiny toy to them now from this height. The most striking part of the immediate view are the wide train lines, all converging together, carving in and out of the city. Another brown transport track running like the river.

'I wonder how far you can see on a really clear day,' Taylah says, 'if it ever is perfectly clear.'

'To Windsor,' replies Caleb, holding his personal video-guide screen up to her with that exact fact displayed.

Taylah's brows rise and she nods, knowing how far away it is because they're going there with his parents after the wedding.

Caleb takes shots of the north vista and Taylah heads around to the south-facing side. Loud choral music crescendos through the invisible speakers overtly emphasising the grandeur of this 21st century miracle, a building designed to inspire no less awe than the painted glass light in a Cathedral – or maybe even more, as the sacred sound reminds you you've never stood as close in height to God. The recorded choir drowns out everything around her except an ambulance racing down the streets below. The sirens never seem to end here, just fade in and out of earshot. Taylah looks down to where the blue lights flash, a trained team of ants racing to save another someone.

She looks up again at her eye height. There's a plane. For a split second Taylah can't tell if it's going, as it should be, or if it is coming. The white aluminium glints in the light and the ambulance sirens below suddenly sound premature, like they knew. And Taylah knows it's heading for the airport, that it's not coming toward her because it simply can't be, the plane cannot be headed for the building she's in – or more accurately *on*, helplessly, fragile, all soft meat and brittle bones and only open sky above them – but her guts turn to ice and her mind flashes to how people felt in the towers that New York September.

Caleb puts his hand on her shoulder, and Taylah turns to him and smiles. She glances back at the definitely-receding plane and wonders if anyone will ever see an aircraft from a building in the same way people did before 2001 again.

***

Passing the Big Ben bell today again, having walked over the bridge, they head north around the side of Parliament. Some men in black suits surround a black car after it pulls into the stately driveway. A guard opens the door and an older man gets out, a grey suit with a briefcase talking on his mobile phone. He nods at the guard holding the car door open and as he walks into the old building the other men clear the driveway. The car swiftly pulls back around into the traffic.

A man next to Taylah wearing a plastic rain poncho takes photos with his silver camera. He leans forwards as he looks through the lens, gripping the camera tightly with both hands even though it's secured on a red lanyard around his neck. His wife readjusts her light scarf and asks him who it was.

'Not sure, love,' he tells her. 'Could be someone though.'

'Dear,' she says and turns away from the fence. 'Can't we see the Abbey now? I want to make the shop before it closes.'

Their accents are a thick English that Taylah and Caleb haven't heard yet. The man tucks his camera back inside his poncho through the neck and takes his wife's hand. They head for the crossing at the traffic lights and nod hello to the police officer standing nearby.

'We should follow them,' she says to Caleb. 'I assume she means where the wedding was.'

'Is it close though?' Caleb looks up at the buildings to see what he can recognise. 'I thought we had to go that way.' He points west along the front of the Parliament and Taylah tells him they can circle back after if they're wrong. The lights change and the crowd in front of them moves across the intersection.

'Maybe I want some Royal memorabilia too.'

Caleb laughs an okay and they follow the other couple.

They come around the old Abbey from the side and walk a few metres away from it so Taylah can turn and get a good shot of the front. Other tourists have the same idea, and they stand in groups hesitating with their cameras while others stand in front of the stairs and get their picture taken. Caleb and Taylah walk further past the others to get the whole of the building in the frame. Two young boys in grey school uniforms walk in front of them. Caleb silently points out their perfect knee-high socks and soft hats, and the boys turn into an old alley on the left.

'We should follow them,' Caleb jokes. 'I wonder where they're going.'

'We can't. We're too old now. We'd get arrested.'

They turn back to look at the Abbey and Taylah takes another few shots.

'Are you positive this is it though?' Caleb says, tilting his head to the side as if the new angle Caleb help him see it. 'It looked way bigger on telly.'

'I'm pretty sure,' Taylah says. 'It's pretty big.'

They walk back towards the doorway.

'You're right though, the stairs do look different.' She squints and pictures the white gowns. The stairs seem at least five rises too small so Taylah looks around, back down the road behind them. 'Is there another entrance?'

A bell rings from the small shop that's lit up to the left of the doorway, and the couple they saw at the Parliament come outside. The wife has a white gift bag in hand. The husband takes his camera out of his poncho and tells her to stand by the door. She smiles and he gets a shot of her in front of the shop.

'Has to be it then,' Caleb says.

They move closer to the store and look in the window at the merchandise. Shelves and tables full of porcelain teacups and handtowels and magnets and decorative plates are lit up under the yellow lights, all embossed with The Queen or Kate Middleton or Diana's face.

Taylah looks outside again. 'It's hard to imagine all those people here.'

***

The wedding happens the next Sunday. Monday is a Bank holiday and everyone in England has it off work, except casuals who even work Christmas, so the whole family has been together since Caleb and Taylah caught the train out from London to Tippley on Wednesday afternoon. Caleb's parents have been here for a fortnight already. They rented an old three storey stone cottage that backs onto the canal from a holiday home website that's big enough for Caleb, Taylah, two of Rachel's friends, and Rachel (before the wedding) too. Most guests have done something similar. Rachel and Kiran don't live in Tippley, they rent much closer to London but weddings in London are entirely unaffordable and they figured everyone had to travel for the big day anyway. Kiran's parents live up North, as do most of his school friends. His university mates are spread all over. Nearly everyone Rachel knows from then still lives back home. She left Australia three years ago, when she was twenty-one, after meeting Kiran on a beach while backpacking across Vietnam, and hasn't looked back since.

'It's still not the same, though, you know,' she said at dinner on Friday night. 'The people are different. The mango is just wrong. And I'm *still* getting used to the bloody weather.'

Caleb's parents Leanne and Andrew had everyone over to the cottage for an Aussie barbeque late on Friday afternoon. They'd spotted a few things at the supermarket, sausages and lamb chops and (tinned, sliced, soaked in sweet vinegar) beetroot, and Leanne made rissoles and lamingtons from scratch. Kiran's dad brought a six-pack of Fosters and they laughed about never having tried it before.

'I don't even think I've seen it in a bottle-o until we got here,' Caleb said.

They didn't sit outside like you normally would because the patio isn't big enough and the weather was wet anyway. Rachel helped her mother in the kitchen coat the little sponge cakes in chocolate and coconut, and Taylah laughed with them about how you can take a girl out of Australia but you can never get Australia out of a girl. Places root in us and we carry the seeds.

***

While the others have marmalade toast and coffee for breakfast, Rachel runs downstairs in her white silk wedding robe and squeals like a six year old at Christmas.

'Jesus Christ, I am getting married today!'

She twirls around the kitchen and they laugh and applaud. Leanne walks over to hug her.

'Congratulations, Rachel,' she says. 'This will be one of the best days of your life.' Leanne squeezes her tighter and thinks of everything that is now to come, a baby boy or a girl and many more reasons for her daughter to fly home.

Andrew walks over to hug his daughter too and Leanne wipes her eyes.

'Oh c'mon Mum, it's too early for that yet,' Caleb laughs through a mouthful of breakfast.

'You're right,' she says to Caleb and turns back to Rach. 'Now what will you eat?'

'Nothing. Everything. Toast!' She laughs and kisses her Dad on the cheek. Coffee is made and Rachel sits beside Taylah at the kitchen bench while her Mum drops two slices of multigrain in the toaster. Rachel and Taylah are the same age. Taylah tries to imagine getting married today. The white dress. The magnetic attention. Rach squeezes her hand, grinning and rocking backwards and forward on the stool.

'I'm going to explode,' Rachel says. 'How do people do this? I'm gonna need a drink before ten o'clock.'

'Eat this and go up and have a bloody shower,' Leanne passes the marmalade over the bench. 'Hair and makeup will be here in an hour and you two,' she points her butter knife at her husband and son, 'better scram. No men around during the beautifying process.'

The toast pops and Rachel jumps up to grab it before her mum can. She finds blackberry jam in the fridge and layers the spread on top. She makes one purple, blackberry slice and one with orange marmalade and takes turns eating the alternate halves.

Caleb stands and stretches, scratching his stomach when his shirt rides up. 'Right,' he says. 'Time for a beer at the Puram's. See you ladies at the ceremony.'

'I'll walk with you,' his Dad says. 'Just give me five minutes.'

Andrew finishes his coffee and kisses Leanne, and hugs his daughter again. Leanne promises to call when they're ready for him to come back. The plan is for Kiran's mother Sonia and the bridesmaids to get ready here, and the men to get ready and pregame the wedding at the Puram's rented place. Then Andrew will come back here for Rachel, and Sonia will go back to her husband and sons when Rachel is ready to head to the hall.

Andrew heads upstairs to grab his suit and Rachel hugs Caleb too.

'Thanks big brother,' she says.

He messes her hair and gives her a kiss on her forehead. 'Anytime, not-so-little sis.'

***

Taylah is the second mint-green bridesmaid in line. Bridesmaid Two. Her dress flows down to just below her knees, and the chiffon straps cross over the back of her shoulders. Her hair was curled and pulled back into a low bun by the hairdresser earlier this morning. The matching gold high heels are half a size too small but she wasn't here to try them on when they were ordered a few months ago. Kiran's younger sister, Maya, is mint-green Bridesmaid One and her dress is the same length but strapless. Kiran's older sister, Reena, is Bridesmaid Three with a high neckline behind Taylah. Rachel's best friend Maid of Honour Maddison brings up the rear. Maddie checks everything in Rach's white handbag, again, refolding the soft tissues and balancing her large bouquet under her arm. Rachel waits in the white limousine idling at the bottom of the steps to the hall with her father. They're talking while the wedding coordinator ensures everything is ready inside. Rachel says the woman's really held her hand through all of this.

Leanne stands under the arch of the first open doorway scrolling through the photos they took on her phone this morning. Her dress is a light, purple lace and the makeup on her eyelids match. The rest of the girls smile quietly at each other as they wait in the entry to the hall, in front of the old closed wooden door, giddy and waiting for the music cue. They rehearsed this yesterday and the day before. The right lyric in the song for the door to open on, the right pace to walk down the aisle, which foot to start with, how much space to give the bridesmaid in front of you, how to hold the bouquet. Rachel said she didn't care that much, really, that she wasn't one of *those* brides, but they all practised anyway. Taylah touches the petals of the white lilies she's responsible for. There are six of them, big open white flowers with light touches of lilac tied together in green ribbon. The ribbons aren't quite the same colour as the Bridesmaids dresses, but they very nearly are the florist said. When she delivered them this morning Rachel made sure to check. Rach picked them out four months ago, after two months of weighing up her options and three private consultations to go over the separate bouquet and ceremony and photo shoot and reception arrangements, ensuring they matched her colour scheme. A white and gold and maybe green Pinterest board didn't really limit anything. She just wanted contemporary-traditional and, for a standard fee, the Cinderella mice team joined the conveyor line and stitched together the Big Day, Her Day, The Happiest Day. The Bridal Table Last Supper display, all for The Bride, her white moment of being Mona in the frame.

Taylah checks the knot in the ribbon and the wedding coordinator silently waves her arms at them like a conductor commanding an orchestra. The car door opens. The processional song starts. The Beatles sing, w*ho knows how long I've loved you.* Taylah steals a quick glance behind her while one of the planning staff opens the wooden door to the ceremony hall. Rachel smiles at her father as he helps her out of the car. The lead photographer captures the rush of white adrenalin. Her green eyes sparkle through her veil and the long lace gown spills out onto the cobblestone ground around her hidden legs. She half turns, pulling the train of her dress out behind herself and smiles coyly at the camera. She is a vision. Her father beams beside her and Leanne sighs at the top of the stairs. Maddie wells up as she closes the tiny white handbag, and Maya beams as she starts walking forwards in front. The guests in the hall all stand at once and turn to face the bride and her party. There are seventy-six people packed into the old hall. Taylah counts Maya's steps and after six, when the music grows slightly louder and The Beatles sing *I will* for the first time, she smiles and walks forward into the room.

The hall is an old converted barn on a hobby farm and the ceiling soars like a cathedral. Wooden beams run up to its peak and dark timber benches, like pews, lie in rows along the floor. Lavender hangs from the benches along the dark carpet aisle, tied in white and green ribbon bundles. The second photographer crouches ahead at the top of the aisle and slightly to the right of the celebrant. Taylah keeps her steps timed to the slow beat of the song, looking to Caleb in his suit at the front, and at the end takes her place next to Maya. Reena smiles when she gets to the front too, turning to take her position. Maddie comes next with the handbag of tissues and her Maid of Honour eight-lily bouquet.

Rachel walks slower than all of them, flanked by both her mum and dad, smiling at each person at the end of the aisles, half-avoiding looking at Kiran until she gets closer and half not being able to take her eyes off him. Kiran smiles at the sky and the photographer captures the shot. The bride stops at the front of the crowd. Her dad, damp-faced, lifts her veil and gently lowers it behind her. Maddie steps forwards to fix the bottom of the veil and take Rachel's bouquet. She holds both bunches of flowers proudly out in front. Her father takes his place next to his wife, wiping his eyes, and Kiran beams as he takes Rachel's hands in front of everyone. The music quietens and the celebrant welcomes everyone to the wedding. Her microphone squeals for a second as the crowd sits back down. A young girl near the front covers her ears with both hands and looks up, cross, at her mother. Taylah looks over to Caleb. He's standing between the Best Man and Kiran's younger brother, in a matching black suit and purple pocket square. He raises his eyebrows and smiles at her. None of the men have seen the bridesmaid dresses yet. Everything was top secret. Next to Caleb, the Best Man taps the front of his suit to check that the rings are still in his jacket pocket. His brow unfurrows slowly and his face relaxes back into a calm, concentrated look. He has the box. The photographer's camera snaps again from the front of the aisle and Kiran fumbles in his pants pocket for his vows. Rachel laughs out to the crowd.

'Rachel,' Kiran says, his voice wobbling. He looks up into her eyes and takes a slow, deep breath. 'Rachel. I love you. I thank God every day that you said yes. Today, you've made me the happiest man alive.'

The crowd sighs and Kiran's father passes his wife a hanky.

'I vow to always love you. I vow to treat you with respect. I vow to always put the kettle on in the morning, and try to make you laugh, and let our children grow up eating vegemite.'

Everyone laughs. Rachel laughs the loudest, nervously, and Kiran takes her left hand. Maddie balances both bouquets in one hand and holds Rachel's written vows ready for her in the other, but Rachel has memorised them anyway. Rachel starts before Maddie passes them forward, so Maddie holds still in her pose, tilting her face slightly skyward on the off chance any stray tears make her waterproof makeup run.

'Kiran, you are the best man I have ever known. You are kind, and funny, and handsome, and loving you is the easiest thing I've ever done.'

Taylah smiles at Caleb, and he smiles back quickly before looking again at Rachel. They've only seen each other in person twice over the past three years, since Rachel moved away, and they haven't lived in the same house since he was twenty. He used to talk about her like she was an impulsive child. Taylah has found that she and Rachel have a lot in common. Now Caleb looks at his sister with pride, as if seeing her as a real person for the first time today, on her wedding day.

Rachel vows to love, cherish, support, and hold Kiran closely for the rest of their lives. The Best Man remembers the rings. Rachel and Kiran slide gold onto each other's fingers. They kiss for the first time as husband and wife. They grasp each other and beam at the audience. Everyone stands and claps and cries and the photographers capture everything.

'I'm finally a Puram,' Rachel laughs, and Kiran's parents welcome her with a hug into the family.

Both parents and parents-in-law kiss their children and walk behind them down the aisle. Rachel and Kiran link arms and kiss people in the crowd on their way out. The bridal party follows, and Caleb wraps his arms around Taylah's shoulders. Maddie keeps her eyes on Rach, prepared to fix her veil as needed and keep everyone from stepping on the dress. Everyone gathers together in the entryway as the newlyweds head down the stairs. Kiran opens the limousine door and Rachel waves to her guests as she climbs in. Kiran picks up the bottom of her train and laughs as he passes it inside the car. He runs around to other door and waves again to his audience. They're all going to see each other again in an hour, when the newlyweds have finished a private photo shoot, but they go through the goodbyes anyway for the sake of capturing the afternoon light. The photographers move to the bottom of the stairs, one facing back up to the crowd and the other with eyes on the couple. The wedding coordinator appears again in the driveway in front of the limo and waves at the driver, giving him his queue. The long white car slowly pulls away from the hall and they wave them into their future.

***

Chocolate cake is distributed by the wait staff after Kiran and Rachel slice into it once together. Beer and wine are bottomless. Kiran and Rachel Puram dance their first dance. They waltz slow circles across the smooth floor to the music, the black suit and white dress blurring almost into one, surrounded by everyone. At the end of the song the edges of the crowd break and spill onto the dance floor. The fathers and daughters, mothers and sons hold each other and sigh about how fast time passes. How quickly everyone grows up.

Once the ceremonial dances are done the DJ cranks the volume. Tea light candles flicker around the edges of the room on the windowsills and white clothed tables. A glass of red wine spills at the back. The flowers start to drop their petals and wilt. A balloon dances on the ceiling, its white ribbon tail having let go of the larger bunch it belonged to. When the DJ shifts the music into this decade Kiran's aunts and grandmother sit together at the table closest to the dance floor, nodding their heads to the quick bass. People spin and laugh and pose for the photographers. Rachel dances in the middle of the room, holding the long train of her dress up with both hands so she doesn't fall over it. Her bare feet slide across the floorboards. Maddie has taken her shoes off too, and made sure to put both pairs safely under their seats. She sways next to Rachel, pink lipstick fading around the edges, still holding tight to her bouquet. Rachel did the bridal bouquet toss earlier but Maddie didn't catch it. One of Kiran's cousins did, nineteen year old Asha. Now it lies across the top of Asha's handbag on a table near the back of the room. Leanne and Andrew dance near Kiran's parents on the edge of the dance floor. Kiran jumps behind Rach with his brother and the other groomsmen. He's left his suit jacket at the bridal table and his bowtie hangs undone around his neck. They've made sure he hasn't been without a beer all night.

When the DJ finally calls last drinks into the microphone at 11:45, Caleb leaves Taylah on the dance floor to find two more glasses of wine. She's stuck to the bubbly to avoid a headache tomorrow. It's a still-alive old wives' tale that somehow, sometimes, seems to work. Dancing with Rachel and her friends, the song changes to one she doesn't instantly recognise and Taylah feels self-conscious for a moment. She pictures herself as others see her – how her arms move, if her hips are in time, what her hair looks like now from the back, if she seems like one of those free people who smile and don't care and genuinely dance like the feel-good sayings tell you to. And then she recognises the tune, something she loves, a song they all love, and she lets go and leans into the music. Under the lights, amongst all the sweating people, she's alone – a self-contained entity, not a pair, not one half of something, not someone to be introduced second or led around the dancefloor, moving backwards. Tispy, she tastes something. A hint of some feeling she wants. Forgetting any others, she is herself as she wants to be. The song ends. She shakes it off.

Taylah smiles at the still-dancing girls and moves to the edge of the dance floor. Caleb spots her and brings over the two glasses. The wine is pink and the bubbles don't rise as quickly as they did four hours ago. A sparkling rosé. They clink their glasses together before drinking and Leanne comes over to join them. Caleb offers to get her a glass too but she says that she's had enough. She sits down on the chair beside them. Purple eye shadow still shines on her eyes. Gold flecks in the colour catch the light.

'She is happy, isn't she,' Leanne says.

'Yeah Mum,' Caleb says. 'She is.'

He pulls up a chair beside her and wraps his right arm around her shoulders. Through the dancing crowd they catch glimpses of Rachel, singing and smiling. Kiran kisses her again.

The first time Rachel came back to Australia was when she came back for a Christmas, and the second was for Maddie's first wedding. She didn't come back for the quick divorce because Maddie travelled to her. Leanne and Andrew have only seen Rachel once more than that since she left home. They flew over nine months after Rachel moved out. That was the first time they met Kiran too, in real life. They'd Skyped a lot before then. Especially at first, when Rachel moved so suddenly to live with a man she'd met in Vietnam. They made her promise she would.

***

When they arrive back home at the cottage they say goodnight to Caleb's parents in the entryway. Leanne smiles and takes her high heels off as they talk, and Andrew says he'll see them all in the morning. Caleb and Taylah head up the stairs to bed. Halfway up Caleb remembers his future hangover and he bounds back down to the kitchen for two glasses of cold water. Taylah stops on the first floor to brush her teeth and Caleb joins her with the water to do the same. They face the mirror and Caleb reaches across her for his blue toothbrush. Taylah passes the toothpaste too and swaps places with him so he can use the sink. The white foam lathers in her mouth and she washes the minty taste around. She gathers the foam on her tongue and spits into the sink, rinses her brush, and opens the tiny bottle of green mouthwash on the bench. She gargles it with her head back and Caleb spits his toothpaste into the sink. He passes on the mouthwash, opting for a mouthful of water straight from the tap instead.

When he's done he rinses his brush and taps it three times on the edge of the sink, as always, to flick the excess water off. With a fresh kiss on Taylah's cheek he takes the water up to their room on the third floor. Taylah stays to wash her makeup off and take the pins out of her hair. The light over the vanity shines bright across the room. She leans close to the mirror and squints at her reflection. She looks tired.

She wonders for a second, Caleb already heading to bed, whether the time and money spent in this position makes any bit of difference. The clock on the shower radio behind her glows a green 1:17. The hot water takes a minute to warm up, so she holds her right fingers under the running tap and reaches for the blue facecloth on her left. It's hanging on the towel rail where she left it to dry this morning.

Caleb takes off his shoes on the floor above and Taylah warms her facecloth under the water. Leanne runs the water in her bathroom too, the simultaneous thunk of the old tap in the wall and reduced water pressure marking their mirrored evening, both women separately looking into their reflections together. Taylah leans into the sink and holds the hot cloth over her face. Water runs down her chin and soaks the front of her hairline. She presses the fabric into her eyes. Mascara moves in smudged lines.

The face wash lathers easily and she carefully rubs it up her cheeks to the bottom of her eyelashes. Small, slow circles in opposite directions like her mother taught her when she was twelve. Gently on the skin. Don't pull downwards or you'll get wrinkles. Always lift it up. She covers her whole face with the soap and the thick liquid turns from orange to white.

As she goes through the routine she rehearses her future wedding day: the moment her family and friends and so-soon-to-be husband see her for the first time, gaze fish-faced as she walks towards them in *that dress* (the white wrapping chameleon morphing with trends and time) – and no mobile phones at the ceremony, she thinks, mind stirring to those disastrous photos of aisles lined not with loved ones but the backs of recording iPhones. She wants to see their real faces looking at her, seeing her not as she is in this mundane life but as the vision she'll be after the labour of her engagement.

When the soap is all washed off she pats her face dry with another towel, wipes on toner and rubs in night oil and finishes with a layer of thick night moisturiser. Her eyes still have slight smudges of black but the rest of the makeup is gone. Her hair has stayed in its low curly bun all day, secured with a bucket of bobby pins and a whole can of hairspray. She finds most of the pins and pulls them out gently. She doesn't bother finding a hairbrush. The curls loosen between her fingers. The hair underneath is soft and untangles easily. Layers on top that copped most of the hairspray stick like fine sandpaper. It needs to be washed out. That will have to wait until morning. Taylah hangs the facecloth back up on the towel rail and turns the light off on her way out.

Caleb scrolls through his Facebook feed on his phone while Taylah takes off her dress and joins him in bed. Her feet are red from the heel straps and when she lies down they get pins and needles. Caleb shows her the photo his sister posted – her and Kiran kissing in a garden at the end of the night, all white dress and black suit and fairy lights, getting a good shot up first and kindly opening the door for everyone else to post their own pictures tomorrow – then he keeps scrolling, so Taylah turns to her journal on the bedside table and writes something quick about tonight.

> *Good:*
> *Rachel was beautiful and happy*
> *Kiran was happy*
> *their parents and family and friends were happy*
> *Everything was so beautiful*
> *the music was great*
>
> *Bad*
> *It was just a bit…*
> *I don't even know*
> *Everything happened very quickly*
> *The coordinator was quite stern*
> *I think I saw her double-check Rach's name on her run sheet*
> *It was very *here she is* *look at her* *becoming a woman* *best day of her whole life**
> *until of course you have kids, and even then…*
> *but it wasn't actually bad,*
> *it was just like every other real wedding I've seen*
> *Probably very expensive*

She glances back over her shoulder to Caleb. She thinks about that breath-taking first moment – their breaths, seeing her – and what his vows will say, how he'll wipe a well-timed tear and shake just a little taking the handwritten lines out of his pocket. The perfect spontaneity of the whole event, the kisses, dancing, cake.

> *Change:*
> *not the tight ship coordination*
> *or having all the same things that everyone else has had*
> *or done just because*

Taylah puts the book down with the pen and turns off her bedside light, overcome with wanting the rite but still thinking she doesn't know how to make this big dream a sure thing. When she moves towards Caleb in the sheets he plugs his phone into the charger and rolls over to face her.

'Hello clean face,' he whispers and puts his hand on her cheek.

'Tonight was fun.'

'Mum drank so much.' He laughs and rolls onto his back.

Taylah lays her head on Caleb's chest and kisses his skin. He runs his hand over her tangled hair and tucks it back behind her ear.

'Sleep now,' he yawns.

'Sleep forever.'

Caleb rolls back again to turn the lamp off and checks the time again on his phone.

'At least until midday,' he says, and pulls the blankets up.

CHAPTER 6

The only way in is up. Up is the only way at all.

From the dark car park to the shiny top floor fishbowl, a single escalator turns itself over to lift Home Makers into the glossy dream. The entrance stands alone, a moth-light for the flooding customers. There is no downwards escalator along this edge of the building nor any static cement staircases offering both up and downward movement. There's just one way to be moved. Park the car. Pause mid-step for the electric sliding doors. Ascend the quiet escalator. Keep your feet balanced between the yellow lines. Let the mess of real trees and sunlight beyond the windows on the second floor you're bypassing disappear behind you. You're not allowed on that floor yet. Keep your face turned upwards. Stride off the escalator. Take a blue bag and yellow trolley. Welcome to homemaking heaven. Welcome to IKEA.

***

When the stair ride ends and the polished top floor opens up, you can press on straight ahead and plunge into the first series of model rooms or you can hang a left and queue up at the restaurant-cafeteria between the looping silver cordons with your disinfected tray. No matter the hour, this first section of floor always jams. Stumped by the need to make a decision so soon after the warm, responsibility-free up-is-the-only-way embrace, and the sudden noise and the other people and the baby always crying, the end of the escalator bottlenecks. There's a hesitation between the lure of the first display and someone's suggestion that the food hall may be terribly busy later on.

On Saturday, a young couple with a quiet toddler ascend into the scene: the father in a blue jumper and loose shorts, the mother with a high ponytail in black Lycra and coral kicks, both with large takeaway coffees. She holds the child and he locates a large trolley and the kid is slid into the top seat, her grey dress and palm-sized pink shoes still in place. They don't hesitate at the first whiff of tepid salmon and potato but push through a crowd of mothers and teen daughters doing the *now or later?* The ponytailed woman presses a button on her black wristwatch, checking her commencing step count on the built-in pedometer, and they push their baby over the first floor arrow into a lounge room scene.

Caleb and Taylah come in the afternoon once they've eaten at home. They bickered after their last overindulgence, on meatballs and mash and steamed veg and bread rolls and cider and jelly and hot chips. They agreed this time they'd be better off avoiding the blind haze that cheap feasting can bring on. Taylah's temper shortens and Caleb turns a spendthrift. Last month they bought two water jugs and a woollen blanket and three cardboard magazine holders that are too small for anything except those expensive niche A5 zines. They're now flattened in the hallway cupboard with some potentially useable batteries and a knot of cables. The jugs are still in their plastic wrap but the blanket, at least, hangs over the back of the lounge. It's unravelled at night-time when neither of them can be bothered to walk into the next room for socks.

At the top of the escalator Caleb takes a yellow bag off the rack and they move on. The first section sign, *Living*, marks the inner entrance. They follow the floor arrows through the six main mock-up areas. *Living*, *Dining*, *Kitchen*, *Bathroom*, *Bedroom*, and *Outdoors*. There are smaller spaces within these, and downstairs is a free for all covering everything from light bulbs to soft-close drawers, but the top floor is what the crowds come for. The apartments and little houses. The stylised rooms you don't just walk through but sit inside, lounge room to lounge room and Mid-Century to Scandi to Art Deco, drawing yourself into each one like trying different jackets before a change room mirror.

***

The first living room to the left of the main walkway features a rich dark leather three-seater. It stands in the centre, holding the room together on a red low-pile Persian rug. Caleb and Taylah don't hesitate to enter. They loop the room once then sit on the left end of the lounge. A glossy black entertainment unit fills the wall facing them and to their left, behind the matching leather armchair, are three identical bookcases dotted with Swedish novels and hard cover cookbooks. Taylah turns her head to look around the three walls. Another couple peer inside from the walkway and Taylah leans back into the chair, hanging her arm over the side. Caleb gets up to look at the cabinetry. A large television stands on the left end of a long floor cabinet, symmetrically mirrored by the wall unit above it in the same dark timber. Two women walk behind the lounge. Caleb runs his fingers along the bottom of the cabinet. He presses at the ridge in the timber and a small door swings open in front of his face.

'Nice,' he says over his shoulder. 'Doesn't need any knobs.'

'You're a knob,' Taylah grins.

Her fingers brush the plastic price sheet attached to the lounge and she pulls it up into view. Thirteen hundred dollars and well out of their price range – not that that really dulls the experience. Caleb pops the other three doors open and closes them again with his fingertips, testing the yellow promise hanging from the roof near the walkway that the unit needs only *the lightest touch*. A couple, early forties, both blonde and in jeans, walk into the same room. An older greying man follows them in. One woman walks between Taylah and Caleb, running her hand along the top of the leather chair. Her partner smiles at the older man and tilts her head, nodding him into the room. The grey man pulls a loose thread from his jumper but doesn't move his feet.

'This one's good, Dad,' the first woman calls across.

Taylah drops the price tag back over the arm rest.

'Not bad,' the bloke says. He offers his daughter a smile.

'Leather,' she says, 'and a high back, so you could fall asleep in it, no worries about your neck.'

The man rubs his neck now she's mentioned it and his daughter pats the top of the chair. He complies this time, walking across to sit down, shooting a quick glance around the room as he does. Caleb faces out to the walkway, angling his gaze out of their bubble. Two middle aged women with trolleys walk past without stopping, and a child runs after them to catch up.

'How's that?' the woman asks her father.

He slides his palms down the length of the rounded arm rests and pushes his head back into the seat.

'Pretty good,' he says, giving Taylah a smile.

Taylah returns it and stands up to join Caleb at the push-open cabinets. She touches the plastic peeling off the TV screen and the second blonde woman points at a second sign hanging from the roof, her mobile in hand.

'Thick grain leather, Glen. Ages gracefully they reckon.'

The older man laughs. 'We're a match made in heaven.'

The daughter checks the price tag. 'Well,' she says, 'it's a start.'

A short, dark haired woman in heels stops outside on the walkway and takes a photo of the room on her phone. Taylah stands behind Caleb, tiptoeing to rest her chin on his shoulder for a second, then they head for the room opposite. Another young couple and two other mothers with yellow trolleys take their place.

***

After the first three rooms in *Living* the path circles an open display of about two dozen lounges. Another five different living rooms continue on the left side of the path. People weave in and out of one after the other, doing the rooms first and doubling back through the lounges or zigzagging across it all like ants before the rain.

A group of teenagers, three girls and a boy, lope around the open display. They test every seat. IKEA has free Wi-Fi and the food is cheap and photos taken here score plenty of likes.

The boy sits in a corner section of a grey sofa, stretching his long legs out along the chaise end. One hand scrolls his phone screen as he talks to the dark haired girl sitting on the footstool in front of him.

'No, not Brayden,' he grimaces without looking up.

'You just don't know him like I do,' she says and stands, hiking her athleisure tights up with both hands, stretching the fabric towards her navel.

The other two girls, both yellowing shades of blonde, sit talking behind the others, faces close. One pulls absentmindedly at the end of her ponytail. She nods and raises her eyebrows while her friend, in green, speaks quickly and snaps the white cotton bra strap escaping down her arm back up onto her shoulder. The other girl joins them, sitting close on the left and leaning into their conversation. The boy turns his head. He rolls over the back of the lounge onto the floor, the knees of his tight jeans collecting dirt. He piles into the middle, lying across them. The girl on the right takes a photo, stretching her arm out into the air at a well-practised angle, fitting all four faces into frame.

***

There are two living rooms in the first corner of the building, both large and well-lit with cherry-picked trimmings and lush rugs running each floor. The first has blue painted walls, not a deep or electric colour but the sort of shade cashmere couples decide between on Saturday mornings after a takeaway macchiato, fanning out the Carolina and Moonstone and Celadon paint cards at arms-length and tilting their heads in the same direction. The mismatched sofas, one light and one a darker grey, square off to a white fireplace. Three gold candles and a ceramic bowl dot the low timber table in the centre. A tall floor lamp is switched on at the side. In the showroom light it's a room of no arguments and tinsel at Christmas, floating in the vanilla imaginary of coastline living where the seasons fluctuate like a light breeze, where year round bare feet appreciate the smooth timber, and red wine is easily cleaned out of the rug. Two young women, mid-twenties, one with black glasses and the other with long auburn hair talk on one of the lounges about work contracts, a burnt-salmon cushion squeezed between them. A boy in blue overalls rearranges the table candles while his parents discuss the floorboards in the next room. He slides them around like a magician with a disappearing ball until mum and dad are ready to move on. A man answers a call as he runs his finger along the top of the fireplace, confused and then alarmed, and an older woman checks her face in the mirror as her partner measures the length of the rug with steady footsteps. All in this duck-egg blue IKEA living room on a cold day in June, while the escalator turns itself over and the lunch queue shuffles through with their beige, sprayed cleaned trays. Fake living rooms being lived through.

The second room has cream walls. The floors are a darker, ashy timber and the television is half-hidden behind a sliding door that's part of a large storage unit. Patterned curtains are drawn over the plain showroom walls, behind a rounded yellow armchair and beside a thigh-high timber bookcase. The books in the bookcase are classic fiction paperbacks, old novels opened just enough that the spines are cracked but the pages aren't dog-eared or tea stained. Kerouac, Poe, Austen, Twain. *Moby Dick* lies flat on the top of the case beside two empty vases. The green cover is a gentle push in the eye line of people tall and old enough that they have both the money for the shelving and the feeling they really should have read Melville by now.

A girl sits in the yellow armchair while her mother paces slowly around the room. The iPad in the girl's lap acquires more fingerprints as the cartoon boy on screen runs faster through coconut trees. Her feet dangle off the end of the chair, undone shoelaces falling to the ground like half-dropped spaghetti. Her mother slides the cupboard door over the unplugged TV, then pauses and lets the screen out again. She notes the board game on the black shelf, the pot plant, the plush blue toy horse. She turns to face the room from the corner where she can drink it all in at once. Her daughter glances up, a reflex after losing track of her mother's position in her periphery, and asks her what the answer to seven times three is. The lava from the volcano is coming through the trees, and the cartoon boy needs to answer the sum to make a skateboard from the coconuts and get to the beach where it's safe from the eruption. The girl frowns and counts on her fingers. Twenty-two is wrong but she types in twenty-one in time. The boy smiles. Coconuts drop. A skateboard fashions on screen. The lava bubbles into the scene, and the boy jumps onto the tree-branch and fruit-wheeled board, long arms flailing, laughing his way down the hill and the clouds part, the lava recedes. She throws her tiny head back, triumphant. Her mother smiles, now behind her, and collects the room and the moment like a yellow balloon in her memory. A new balloon added to the future bunch of what home can be like, under these lights and away from the mess of everything outside the shop doors, just the two of them.

***

Now: do you buy a round or a rectangle dining table?

The process is quite complex. The *Dining* section is different to *Living* – it's more open, like a showroom usually looks, with clinical lighting and visible price tags and no wallpaper or art running the white walls so you really notice that they haven't bothered with a ceiling. The spread of tables and dining chairs, more than eighty settings in an uneven grid across the slick grey floor, come before the playrooms do, because the done up dining rooms bleed into the *Kitchen* sections, and people rarely have formal dining rooms in their houses here anymore. We can't afford the space. The main pathway carves down the middle of the forty-odd sets. Forty white, brown, timber, plastic, glass, and chrome-plated tables to walk between, sit down at and rearrange chairs around. The hottest style is extendables; drop-leaf tables where both ends pin underneath and can be brought out again for a doubled length, for people who have friends but also a room that is too small to have to shimmy along the wall every normal morning. The square and oval tables are set up in the far corners of the room, plainly, with standard white or timber chairs, biding their time until it's their season to be 'in.' It's a circle and rectangle year.

The most eye-catching table is on the right side of the path. A long, light timber piece with an ashy veneer that's twice the width of most others. An entertainer. You can imagine the platters lining it and the guests all crowded around the edge, glasses full and the host (you), a delight.

***

Caleb and Taylah half-heartedly weave through the hundred open plan table sets, mostly sticking to the path and talking about Taylah's brother instead of the furniture. Brett sent her a selfie with their Labrador Teddy at 11 o'clock last night, meaning he's gone back up home to see their folks and has probably split up with his boyfriend.

'Mum didn't say anything when we spoke this week,' Taylah says, her eyes skirting over the dining chairs that run the far right wall.

'Maybe it was a spontaneous trip,' Caleb offers across a dark table.

Taylah looks at the photo again. 'He looks pissed.'

'Drunk you mean?'

She nods.

'A spontaneous dumping, then?'

They reach the end of the open tables and head into the first *Dining/Kitchen* room. The dining table is first, a white leg and pine top rectangle with a bench seat running the walkway side and simple white chairs dotting the other edges. A woman with a trolley blocks the room around the left side of the table. She leans onto the back handle of her shopping trolley, not a little blue one you drag behind you with the IKEA bag hung over the top but the same big ones you use at the grocery store. She flips through the latest store catalogue trying to figure out if this is the table she liked and, if so, why it looks so different to the pictures. It's not the one on page 60 or the one on 64. She tries page 63 again, checking the name in the glossy book against the Swedish name on the table and doing an excellent job of not noticing the young couple hovering by the back wall artwork who are trying to look at shelving she's stopped next to. The girl runs her fingers through her long, black hair. Her boyfriend pulls one of the chairs out from under the table and, after a second, slides it back again. He waits and the woman doesn't move, and Taylah and Caleb go on to the kitchens.

The first kitchen is white drawers and pine bench tops, an oversized white ceramic sink and yellow curtains and a butler's pantry with a second, silver sink so the mess is always away and the person that washes the dishes is away too. The second dining room is in muted tones, black gloss table and dark floors and grey walls and dim light in the kitchen. The third is bright again, whites and blues, and Taylah likes it so she opens all of the cupboards and drawers, tries the unhooked silver tap, turns the pages on the open display cook book to a glazed orange cake recipe and leans on the bench, pressing her palms into it. She looks out to the walkway like a matching lounge room is there too, with blue cushions and framed photographs on the wall, and four bedrooms and two cars and a patio outside to the left, two kids and a cat or a dog. Caleb puts his phone away and moves into the next room. The dining set is a glossy black again but the kitchen is stark. LED lights. Clean lines. Induction plates built into the stone bench top. A white sign hanging by the electronic lighting panel says this is a kitchen where you can *cook smarter*. The next, a thin pokey room with exposed brick wallpaper and every possible utensil hanging from hooks and rails along the walls suggests you *make small storage more fun*.

The last kitchen is *raw food friendly*. Silver pots of plastic chillies and herbs are fixed to the wall. The tiny signs glued into the polystyrene soil read Basil, Coriander, Lemon Balm, Parsley.

'Ka-tie,' Caleb says, dragging out her name and standing in the middle of the room.

Taylah smiles. Her friend Katie has jumped on the raw food craze, which everyone knows because there's a new photo up of her greenery every second day. She's transformed her kitchen – after a trip to IKEA no doubt – which means having a corner bench that's conducive to growing tiny plants inside because you live in an apartment or think that cleaning soil off the kitchen bench every now and then sounds much easier than actually learning to garden.

'We'll be having some raw food at dinner in two weeks, no doubt,' Taylah says.

Caleb grabs a wooden spoon from the cylindrical silver holder next to the sink. He swings it like a cricket bat, following through with a squint into the distance and shielding his eyes from the dream sun with his right hand. 'I absolutely cannot wait.'

***

When Taylah comes here alone, after work on school days when Caleb is late in the city or on weekends when he's out with friends, doing the top floor is a different business. Sometimes she sends him photos as she goes through of all the things she likes. Sometimes she doesn't. When she eats she sits in the middle of the cafeteria, rather than off to the side near the big windows or down in the corner where it's quiet. In the middle are screaming children who knock their tiny, bright painted chairs over and mashed potato falls from their faces to the floor. Their mothers try to shush them for a while until they just can't do it anymore and the kid is left to terrorise the wooden toys, throwing them across the floor into the aisle where they wait like lazily-planted landmines. And they keep screaming. Taylah tries to fix her expression into an understanding face, an it's-okay face even when she's dying inside to yell at them to stop. And when she can't manage it anymore or is sufficiently unconvinced at her own attempts at empathy, she scrolls through the newsfeed on her phone or looks out the big windows at the grey sky until she's finished her small serving of meatballs and lingonberry jam. When Caleb is there they hold hands between mouthfuls and laugh at themselves eating here, laugh at how funny it is to eat meatballs and play in houses and how lovely and sweet the day. It's a close and romantic thing. Without Caleb there are sticky tables and parents ignoring their children and wooden blocks on the floor and the food is colder and the din echoes, and you notice it. Caleb is a warm blanket and white noise and the rose tinting on her right-side-of-the-highway glasses.

And when she gets home she writes,

> *I rushed through the kitchens in IKEA today*
> *Normally I hang around in them*
> *But I feel 100% less domestic alone*

not bothering to mark up the Good, Bad, Change.

***

Another couple join Taylah and Caleb in the bathroom. They are older by a few years, impeccably dressed, and the woman is heavily pregnant. They rotate around the white room like repelling magnets. Caleb notes the man's tailored trousers and leather shoes. The pregnant woman leans against the long marble bench top and tells her partner it's perfect.

'This is what we need,' she says.

He walks around the small room once, checking the flow, and then crouches in front of the sink.

'Okay,' he says, standing. 'It will fit.'

They leave, the woman rubbing her belly, and Taylah and Caleb emerge from the shower. They head across the pathway into the next bathroom – a cream and green creation. Two ladies are already inside. The younger one, mid-thirties, sits on the edge of the bathtub with her legs crossed over one another while her mother, early 60s, attends to her lipstick in the mirror.

'I just don't like the way Jason treats you,' the mother says.

'I like the lights,' says Caleb, pointing above the mirror from the aisle.

The daughter shrugs.

Taylah nods, silently agreeing with Caleb. He walks inside the bathroom and into the shower again. It's an open set, not a closed cubicle, and the enormous silver showerhead suspends from the ceiling. The other women don't look up.

'The storage in here is excellent,' says the mother, putting her coral lipstick back into her black handbag and opening the tall cupboard to her left.

'Jason is my husband,' the daughter sighs and moves into the shower, fiddling with the silver taps and running her fingers along the diamond tiles on the wall.

'I like this one,' Caleb says.

'Same,' says Taylah.

'You're right,' the daughter agrees. 'The storage in here is excellent.'

***

They want a bath in their future home. Not just any bath. Not a built-in rectangular corner tub to wash children in after long days spent outside in the grass, scrubbing the taste of worms from tiny pink mouths. An adult bath. A cold water on summer afternoons bath. Taylah finds one she likes in bathroom number four. The room is black and white: white subway tiles on the wall, white cabinets with black handles, black towel rails, black toilet paper holder, monochrome diamond tiles on the floor. A green plant sits on the windowsill. The bath is an old style, claw foot tub on the left wall of the room. Black on the outside. White on the in. Taylah lets go of Caleb's hand when they walk into the room, and when the other couple also in there leave she climbs inside the tub. She smiles up at Caleb and he crouches down next to her, seeing her how it would be: in the steam, jeans-less. Wet white skin and blonde hair catching the light. He takes Taylah's hand and asks her if she likes it. She closes her eyes and smiles, then motions for Caleb to hop in. It's less about liking it and more about whether it feels right. That's how this whole thing works. Get inside it. Feel it out. Draw the material into your life, room by room by room. Interior design doesn't just define a time but shapes and creates it, framing the way we move through our lives. We need these places and we've learned to love to decorate, so space is sold to us and time is sold to us, and the idea of comfortable love sells big. Caleb looks around the empty bathroom. A lady in a yellow IKEA shirt walks past, holding a clipboard. Caleb calls out to her.

'Excuse me,' he asks with his hand raised. 'There's no sign on this. Which is it?'

'Sorry,' the lady shakes her head and starts walking again. 'We don't actually sell the baths.'

*****

Outdoors is the last section. Here it's not upstairs with all of the other faux living on Level 2, bar a few minor exceptions where Juliet balconies and alfresco areas extend from bedrooms or a kitchen, marked with plastic palms and sky-blue wallpaper. The real *Outdoors* comes with the Market Hall. People push in with their trolleys and blue bags full, following the floor arrows once again after an interlude between the near-endless low-shelved aisles and choices of cheese graters, place mats, lampshades, and scented candles. There are so many scented candles most people never leave without one. There are even palm-sized glass bowls of coffee beans spread throughout the area, like department stores leave out in the crowded perfume section before Christmas and on February 13th for people to clear their brains with. People use the beans too, nosing them like they do with the same candles that the strangers before them did and cooing over the scents.

Vanilla Pleasure, Calming Spa, and Fresh Laundry walk out the door. Homemade Gingerbread and Winter Berry are also popular with the crowds in December, despite the fact that half of the country is on fire at this time and no one is ever inside to smell them.

The candles bleed into the fake flowers, and the plastic blooms into real plants that don't require much watering or sun. Little potted succulents. Some of these are fake as well, but they're easy to tell apart with a fingertip that will either resist the brown painted foam or prick on an actual cactus. Following the succulents are taller ferns, hip height leafy foliage whose green rot is a welcome change from the smell of recycled air-conditioning. Then the floor opens out again, and people's shoulders relax as they come into the brighter light. The cement warehouse floor is sporadically covered with squares of realistic turf or acacia decking that locks together like puzzle pieces. Nearly every scene is the same. There's the barbeque in the corner, black and set to run on either gas or charcoal, and some weather-proof shelves or a storage bench. A large wooden table takes centre stage, enough matching seating around it for guests. There are cream fabric parasols and gazebos for people who don't have patios already built in. The Backyard comes together with red cushions and rugby balls, basketball hoops, sun lounges, hammocks, and fairy lights. White-lidded blue eskies dot the designs.

It's an *Outdoors* beyond fake green and grey, that taps into a lifestyle memory of sunburnt childhoods in stinking floral swimmers with cricket bats and dogs that shake the water out of their fur on the grass. It's a sacred space, not the side of the house outside where the wheelie bins go. It's the blooming, lorikeet dotted and kookaburra sound-tracked, Hills-Hoist swinging, sprinkler laughing grass-stained afternoon space flavoured with glasses of red cordial or passionfruit soft drink. A packaged idea accelerating towards a generational memory as apartment blocks rise and this dream land is carved up still in smaller plots.

***

Their pre-agreed shopping plan to not buy anything unless they desperately needed it, because they couldn't think of anything they did need when they set off from home after lunch (excluding the waterglasses and small sheepskin rug now under Taylah's arm), means they've avoided having to try and find anything at the end. They stick to the middle of the final towering aisles, passing people thumbing Swedish names into the locator tablets and looking around desperately for anyone wearing yellow, trying to balance multiple cardboard flat packs on a single low trolley, wondering how they'll fit everything into the car. Before the checkouts are a few last piles of homely accoutrements: bulldog-shaped cushions, striped tablecloths, plastic hand-moulded oven mitts. Caleb puts his arm around Taylah's shoulder and they head past it all for the checkouts. Most lines are the same length. They take their place behind other people who are also only taking what they can carry without buying a bag. Little icings for their individual housing cakes. Taylah runs her fingers through her new fluffy mat. She thinks of how well it will hang over the back of their office chair and soften the whole feel of their lounge room. A $1 hotdog sign glows above them. Taylah smiles up at Caleb. He squeezes her shoulders. The line shuffles forward. The woman two places in front of them tries to slide her yellow trolley back onto the hanger without dropping her casserole dish or membership card she's already taken out of her wallet. She smiles at the checkout worker, a teenage boy with dark eyes who sits on a swivel chair who asks her how her day's been.

'Not bad, thank you,' she says. 'Some more bits and bobs for home.'

She pays. The man in front of Caleb and Taylah places his items and takes out his wallet. The checkout boy asks him how his day has been. The woman scoops her loose items up into her arms and heads for the elevator back down to the car park. Caleb drops his arm from Taylah's shoulder and reaches into his back pocket. Taylah places the items on the belt. The checkouts beep. Receipts print. Yes, their day's not been bad thanks. The checkout boy smiles from his chair and reaches for Caleb's card.

The only way out is through.

CHAPTER 7

In the group chat Katie told everyone dinner was from seven. She read the thread back twice while eating lunch at her desk and once again when she knocked off at half-past five, scrolling through the meal decisions and waiting with the thousand other 5:39 pm Friday commuters. At six-thirty she turns the oven on and pours a glass of nearly-cold white wine, sitting at the kitchen bench with the free lifestyle magazine that came with the junk mail in the post. Rob reminds her, coming out of their bathroom in a towel, one hand finger-combing his wet hair and the other clutching a half-empty bottle of beer, that seven really means eight and they probably won't want to eat until after nine anyway. She thinks of the chicken breasts marinating in thick, sweet sauce in the fridge. A bit longer won't hurt. Rob pulls his jeans on in their bedroom and she lines candles down the middle of their table, ready to be lit.

When the minutes tick over to 7:05, Katie finishes her drink and calls out to Rob over the music playing from the computer in their bedroom.

'Should we chuck the heating on? Or the telly?'

He sticks his head out of the doorway. 'Sorry, what? I'm just making a playlist.'

'Why are you bothering?' she says. 'Just search like, indie up-tempo dinner party songs, and come and help me.' She holds both hands out, repeating her question. 'Heating? TV?'

Rob frowns. 'What do you need help with? No to both.' He disappears back inside the room and changes the song. The music pauses, and Rob calls back. 'Put some more clothes on if you're cold.'

'I'm not cold, I'm just saying,' Katie adds. She runs her arms down the long cotton sleeves of her dress.

'I don't know why you're getting all stressed, babe. Have another drink and relax.'

The wine is slightly colder now. She tests the other two bottles in the fridge door with the backs of her fingers, hoping Jess remembers to bring some red. Six other glasses line up in pairs on the bench.

There's beer in the fridge too, and two bottles of water on the dining table with seven small glasses. Rob was in charge of the booze and Katie prepped most of the main before work this morning – sliced the red and yellow capsicums, the parsley, bay leaf, quartered the lemon, sprinkled the pepper, and poured a tin of organic crushed tomatoes over the ten chicken breasts. She checks on it in the fridge again. Rob tells her to stop opening the door so much as he walks into the kitchen, putting his empty bottle down next to the sink.

'No wonder you're cold,' he says.

'I'm not bloody cold Rob.'

The intercom buzzes. Rob exaggerates his redirection towards it, letting his head flop left as he steps right.

'Yellow,' he grins into the speaker.

'Maaate,' Caleb's voice responds.

Rob pushes the button unlocking the front door to their unit complex. Katie pulls her hair back into a ponytail, tying it up with the band around her wrist and checking it in the mirrored splashback. She checks the oven again. Rob opens the front door and welcomes Taylah and Caleb inside.

'Hey, hi, good to see ya, yeah nah leave your shoes on, you're right,' he kisses Taylah on the cheek and hugs Caleb, slapping his back in the entryway.

Taylah carries two bowls into the kitchen, a blue ceramic filled with yellow rice and a white plastic one of green salad, both covered over with cling wrap. She places them on the bench and drops her handbag and coat on the lounge.

'Hello gorgeous,' Taylah says to Katie.

They hug and Katie takes the open wine bottle from the fridge.

'Nice skirt,' Katie says, pouring Taylah a glass.

'Beer?' Rob asks Caleb, taking the six pack he brought to the fridge.

'Oh, thanks,' Taylah says, placing her palms on her hips. 'It's new.'

'Very nice. Tan is very in this year. And your hair looks so good.'

Taylah tucks her short cut behind her ear. 'Oh, yeah, I've just had it done again. I'm still getting used to it. I kind of miss long hair like yours,' she adds. 'It's so nice.'

'Are we the first ones here?' Caleb asks. He takes a sip from his bottle and raises his eyebrows, looking down at the turquoise label.

'Yeah, Sarah and Dyl shouldn't be far away,' says Katie.

Caleb turns his bottle around and reads the back. 'This is nice mate, new is it? Don't think I've seen it before.'

'Jess'll be late,' Taylah adds, turning her back to the boys.

Katie laughs. 'That's why she's in charge of dessert.'

Rob nods at Caleb, swallowing his mouthful and they sit down apart on the lounge. 'Yeah, a local. Tried it out the other weekend, at Mike's thing in the city. They had it at the shops this arvo so I thought I'd get some.'

'Yeah right, not bad.'

Taylah places her glass down and looks over the two dishes she brought. 'Look at us, we're adulting so hard tonight,' she jokes. She puts the green salad into the fridge and asks Katie for something to cover over the rice, trying to trap the heat in until they're ready to eat.

'We can chuck it in the microwave for a second if we need to later,' she says with her hands hugged around the bowl as Katie takes out a cloth from the drawer. 'It's been cold this week.'

'Do you want the heating on?'

'Nah, nah, I'm alright. Some wine will do me.'

The girls both lean their backs against the kitchen bench, facing out to the rest of the room. Large photographs of Katie and Rob hang opposite them on the lounge room wall: resting together against a palm-tree that sags over a beach sunset, grinning in a sky-scraper city, a red desert scene with Katie sitting straight-backed in a white dress on a picnic rug and three roped camels saddled up behind her. Katie had the pieces canvas printed last Christmas.

Taylah smiles at the photos and says she wishes they had seen more of Dubai than the space-age airport.

Katie smiles too and tells Taylah, again, about the dinner she and Rob had that night out in the desert. The meat and red spices, the belly dancing, the music.

'Speaking of, they had a section in here,' Katie reaches for the magazine she was reading before Taylah and Caleb came in. She flips to the back, past the ten minute morning yoga routine and supplement advertorials to the travel section – two pages on the UAE, white resorts and white mosques and orange desert.

'Wow looks amazing,' Taylah says. 'We'll have to go next time.'

'Definitely. You should go there next year, go to Europe and stay a few nights on the way home.'

'Did you have to cover up whenever you went out though?'

'Yeah nah, not really. I mean the women there fully do.'

'Yeah, right,' Taylah says, looking at the package hotel and flights deals, thinking it over.

'It was fine though. Wouldn't it be the best couple of days,' she leans in to Taylah, 'after you go to like Greece or Croatia and get engaged and then have a little engagement-moon in five star desert luxury.'

Taylah laughs, smacking Katie's arm with the magazine. 'Oh my God, stop.'

'What?' Katie jokes, looking at her own diamond ring. '*I* can say that. You know they need to be led in the right direction.'

Taylah rolls her eyes, thinking she's right, and flips back to the life articles in the middle. 'Listen here, Katie,' she says, reading the page. 'Do you know everything you need to about UTI's? Hey?'

'Oh Christ, no.'

'I'll just save this one for you for later,' Taylah winks, and dog-ears the page.

Taylah pauses on the next page, skimming a piece on Kick-Ass Career Women, and Katie tops up her wine. Rob and Caleb laugh on the lounge at a video on Rob's phone. The intercom buzzes again. Katie lets Dylan and Sarah into the complex.

'Oh, I'm glad Sarah is coming,' Taylah says.

Sarah is Dylan's new girlfriend. He's been seeing her for over a year but they've only recently become dinner-party-invite official.

Dylan and Sarah let themselves inside. They exchange hellos and leave their shoes on. Rob gets Dylan a beer and they talk about the bright label and Taylah pours Sarah a wine. Katie unwraps the cheese plate Dylan carried in and compliments Sarah on her dress. Sarah smiles a thanks and takes a dried apricot from the plate.

'Aren't we a bit povo for figs, Sarah?' Taylah jokes.

Sarah thanks her for the wine and takes the lid off the two dips. A basil and a pumpkin. She cuts some thin slices from each of the white cheeses and, after the girls have helped themselves to some crackers, passes the plate over to Dylan and the other guys.

'How's work going, Sarah?' Katie asks.

'Ah yeah, it's good, thanks,' Sarah says, checking her phone and sliding it back into her handbag. 'We just finished our winter wonderland week today. That was full on.'

'Like a Christmas in July thing?' Taylah asks.

'Yeah pretty much,' she nods. 'We just don't bother putting up a tree. And, honestly, Santa once a year is more than enough.'

The girls laugh and agree.

'Nah, we do all wintery activities and it's quite nice, especially this week. They all came in their little beanies and scarves,' Sarah smiles.

'Oh stop,' Katie laughs.

'That is so cute.'

'You have no idea. Fake snow was the biggest hit.'

'I remember doing that,' Dylan says, bringing the cheese plate back up to the bench. 'We did it in like year two, I think.' He slides the food to the middle of the bench and kisses Sarah on the side of her head.

'Yeah, the kids totally lost their minds.'

'What age group are you in with again?' Taylah asks, slicing more cheese.

'Three to fours.'

'Sounds bloody exhausting,' says Katie.

'Yeah, nah,' says Taylah, shaking her head. 'Well, probably more than my ten year olds.'

Sarah laughs. 'You get used to it.'

'I tell you what takes some getting used to, finding glitter all over the house. Everywhere,' Dylan shakes his head and grins at his girlfriend. 'In the fridge, in the bathroom. Under my fingernails!'

They all laugh and Sarah slaps his arm. 'It's not that bad.'

'So, are you two living together now?' Katie asks after a sip of her wine, shooting a sly grin in Taylah's direction.

'Nah,' Dylan says. He pauses for a half-second, as if to say more, but nods instead and takes three new beers from the fridge, leaves the bottle caps on the bench and joins Caleb and Rob on the lounge.

As the girls all share a look, the light on the oven clicks off and Katie jumps up to place the chicken in, taking the cool glass dish from the fridge and sliding it onto the hot middle rack, setting the timer for thirty-five minutes.

'I tell you what though,' Sarah says after taking another drink of her wine. 'These kids might only be three but they do not miss a beat. I have had that many questions about "the airplanes on TV."'

'Yeah, shit, how horrendous is it,' says Taylah.

'I can't believe it's another one,' Katie shakes her head. 'Not that it's the same, you know, but still.'

'Well, you never know,' Taylah shrugs.

'You'd think that parents would try and stop their kids from watching the news though,' Sarah says. 'I could not believe how many of these kids have seen it and kept talking about crashes and stuff all day. We did not know what to say,' she explains. 'Janet, our centre manager, was just like "keep distracting them with the snow."'

'What were you saying in the car, babe?' Taylah turns around to the lounge. 'About the plane?'

'Oh yeah,' Caleb takes his phone out and types something into the screen. 'Three hundred people they reckon.'

'That's so scary.' Katie folds her arms and looks out her kitchen window.

'Hard to get your head around,' says Rob. 'There's been rolling coverage all day.'

'Rolling stock coverage has been more like it,' Dylan says. 'They can't even get anywhere near the real thing yet.'

'Two in one year.'

'And the same bloody airline!'

'I am never flying with them again,' Taylah says.

'When did you ever?' Caleb points out.

'You know what I mean.'

'Isn't the coincidence crazy though,' Rob says. 'Could have been any airline, but no. Imagine owning the company, how shit would that be.'

They all look to the TV. It's switched off, but it draws their attention anyway. They know what's playing beneath the black. The song changes in the background, a slow guitar strum to electric drums with a few seconds of heavy nothing between tracks. And they keep looking, for a moment, to the black rectangle like keeping the screen off will stop it from being real and the aircraft will only be there, a smouldering wreck, empty seats in a field, passports and blown open suitcases, if they dare press the button on the remote.

'How long do you reckon it'll take for some dried up back-bencher to make this a public lesson about the opposition?' Taylah says.

'Too right,' Caleb laughs.

And that's the extent of it, the continental drift of nation-states a touch of tragedy here, a flavour in the potluck dinner party conversation, as close as we openly stray into politics at this moment in the election cycle and this early in life, this early in the night.

The intercom buzzes and Jess's voice calls out through the speaker.

'Hi, hi, sorry I'm late, idiot driver took me the long way. Let me in. I have wine.'

Rob stands and buzzes her inside the front gate and Jess skids into the room grinning, a package of profiteroles and a small tub of vanilla bean ice cream in her hands, bottles of shiraz under each arm.

***

Once the oven timer has beeped and Katie has checked the chicken, twice, to make sure it's just the red sauce in the dish and the meat isn't actually still pink inside, she announces that they may finally eat. Everyone takes their place at the table. Taylah blasts the turmeric rice dish in the microwave. Jess opens both bottles of wine. Rob sits at the far end, the head of the table with his back to the large window, and the others shuffle around the remaining seats. Caleb looks over to check that Taylah's alright with the rice and sits down opposite Jess. He leaves two seats together free for Taylah and Sarah, both still pottering in the kitchen with the hot parts of the meal. The boys move on from the local beer to Jess's wine. Rob pours everyone a full glass from his head seat and the girls place the hot plates of food between the green salad bowl and the candles.

'Cheers,' Rob raises his wine as Katie sits down beside him.

They all clink glasses across the table, and smile and tuck into the food. The green salad circulates and Sarah comments on the kale and cranberries.

'All organic,' Taylah nods, mostly at Katie, not missing the opportunity to quietly bring up that it cost twice normal price.

'So is everything in the chicken,' adds Katie. 'Herbs from our own little kitchen garden up there.' She points her fork towards the six small pots along the windowsill near the kitchen sink, and everyone turns their heads to acknowledge the efforts.

Taylah passes the pepper and rock salt with the warm rice, saying she didn't want to add it in earlier herself. They lift heaped spoonfuls from the blue bowl and each smile in Taylah's general direction after doing so. Rob slices into his first piece of chicken and croons when it's in his mouth.

'Great chicken babe,' he says to Katie after swallowing. 'Best chicken I've ever had.'

Everyone laughs and agrees it tastes delicious.

Katie frowns and smiles together. 'It's not too dry? It's a bit dry.'

'No, honestly, it's just right,' Taylah says.

***

Jess stands, leaning over the table to top up everyone's glasses of wine with the second bottle, and Taylah asks her how her love life is.

'What love life?' she jokes.

'No one on the radar?' Katie leans in.

Jess rolls her head, not committing to a no.

'Go on,' Taylah prompts.

Dylan asks Caleb if he caught the Swans game last weekend and Caleb reminds him that he went.

'Yeah shit, that's right, I saw that,' Dyl says, remembering liking the picture.

Jess swallows a large mouthful of wine and holds her hands out, shrugging her shoulders, not yet willing to let on. 'Oh, you know,' she says. 'There's always someone floating around.'

Caleb smiles at Jess then nods to Dylan. 'Have you finished your Masters yet, man?'

'Nearly, end of the year I'm done.'

'Yeah right. It's been good then?'

'Yeah it has, yeah.'

Taylah leads Katie, knowing more than one-nighter gossip is lying just under the next glass of wine. '...But?'

Jess laughs. 'Alright, alright. Pass the wine.'

Caleb says to Dylan, 'I might start an MBA next year. Work's good but, you know. You need it to get ahead now hey.'

'True,' Dylan agrees.

'I mentioned it to my folks when they were up and my Mum was all like, "*You've already got a job. What about putting a deposit on a house? Interest rates blah blah,*"' Caleb shakes his head and Dylan laughs with him. 'She is right, but it's way more competitive for us than it was for them. Houses are way more expensive. And fat chance in this town. Knocking over a Masters will help me up the food chain, you know.'

'You'd hope so mate. It's a dog eat dog world alright. You've gotta provide.'

'No joke.'

Sarah brings the open bottle over from the kitchen and Jess tops up her own glass.

'Her name's Jessie,' Jess sighs and nods at the table.

'Jessie?' Taylah asks.

'Yep, Jessie,' she says.

'Jess and Jessie,' Sarah says.

'Jessie and Jessie,' Katie giggles.

'Yes,' Jess sighs. 'I know.'

'So, how did you meet?' Sarah asks.

'On an app, Sarah, like normal people,' she laughs.

'Is it serious?' Taylah asks.

'Um,' Jess says. 'Not really.'

'Yet,' Taylah grins.

Katie sings, 'Jessie and Jessie, sitting in a tree, k-i-s-s-i-n-g.'

Jess half laughs, 'First comes love, sure. Just don't hold your breath for the rest of the song.'

***

Taylah and Sarah wrap up the copious leftovers. Caleb helps Katie stack the plates in the dishwasher. Jess takes out seven bowls for the dessert and carries the tray of profiteroles over to the table. She doubles back for spoons and the ice cream. Dylan divvies out the last of the red wine, and Rob says there's more wine and beer in the fridge. The last wavering flame of the three tea light candles flickers out in a pool of its own making.

Sarah rubs her stomach and says she doesn't know if she can fit anything more in. Taylah laughs and says neither can she, but she's allowed to devour some ice cream on weekends so her new skirt won't stop her. Katie and Caleb return to the table, and Katie checks the label on the cold tub. She turns it over in her hand, looking for the nutritional information.

'It won't kill you, Katie,' Dylan jokes.

'Yeah, no, I know,' Katie shakes her head. 'I just wanted to check.'

'How's the challenge coming?' Jess asks her.

'It starts next week,' she answers, placing the ice cream back onto the table.

'Is it belly or butt this time?' Rob asks, reaching for the profiteroles.

'Booty,' she corrects him.

'Awesome,' Sarah says. 'Are you doing that just down here, at that place everyone's always posting photos from?' She waves her hand in a vague outside direction towards the window.

'No, no,' answers Katie. 'I did the last one there, that ab detox back in May. This one's an online program where you get like a meal plan and the chick posts videos of the workouts and there's a leader board and you just do it at home or at your own gym or wherever.'

'Oh yeah, my friend from work did that,' Taylah adds. 'Or one of those.' She scoops some ice cream in beside her two profiteroles and passes the tub down to Caleb. 'I don't think she won. She said the meals were like, really filling though, and she didn't feel like she was starving or anything so that's good.'

'That is something,' Jess smirks.

'Are you doing the before and after photo shoots then?' Sarah asks with a smile.

Katie nods and hovers her hand over the dessert plate, searching for the smallest one.

Dylan laughs at them. 'Aren't they just like, in the second photo the people have a fake tan and are smiling and standing up straight?'

'Or two totally different people,' Rob chips in.

'No,' Katie says and turns to answer Sarah. 'I'm going to do the before photo and stuff tomorrow.'

'May as well eat up then,' Rob says to her, scooping some ice cream into her bowl after Dylan finishes filling his own. 'Think of the likes.'

'I don't need to look like a bloody white whale,' Katie says.

'Oh, shut up, you so do not,' says Jess, pulling the profiteroles.

'We should all do one soon, it would be fun doing it together,' says Katie. 'Keep each other motivated and these drop-kicks interested in us, the lucky bastards.'

'Egg each other on more like. Who would win?' says Jess.

'That's not the point,' Sarah says.

'What is?' Caleb says.

Rob laughs with his head back. 'Careful, mate.'

***

Jess accepts a beer from Rob now that the red wine is gone. She finishes her last mouthful of red, tipping her head back to reach the dregs, and nods a yes over her shoulder to Rob who's holding open the fridge door. Her fingerprints cloud the outside of the bowl, the foggy marks shining in the lamplight. Sarah declines another drink. She's driving. Outside a police car screams past. The blue and red lights flash into the apartment like a passing disco, on the way to meet strangers caught up in some late event on another street. Rob brings bottles over for Caleb and Dylan without needing to ask, and Taylah and Katie nurse glasses filled almost to the rim with the last of the white wine. Katie had poured them, grinning through Taylah's protests about driving home as she glanced at her wrist, despite never wearing a watch.

'She probably would have convinced him,' Katie adds, finishing a story about a friend of hers from work who's just come back after having her second kid, 'if they'd have had two boys but they've got one of each now, so.'

'Found it,' Taylah interrupts. 'Sorry,' she says to Katie, placing a hand gently on her arm before turning her phone screen around to the group to show them a cheese plate she bought last weekend. 'It's this one.'

'Oh my god, I love it.'

'That is so nice.'

'Yeah I couldn't go past it,' Taylah smiles, zooming into the picture to show off of the detail.

'God, not the bloody plate again,' Caleb jokes.

'Oh stop, it's nice,' Katie says to him.

'You love it,' Taylah frowns at her boyfriend.

'It's ridiculous,' Caleb responds.

'It is not,' Taylah and Jess say in unison.

Taylah continues, mostly to the girls, 'Isn't it perfect though?'

'Yeah, it is,' says Katie. 'Such a great size.'

'Good find,' adds Sarah.

'We need things like this,' Taylah says, more to Caleb this time, 'That's what will make a place feel like ours, all the little things we find together, whenever we can actually buy something.'

'Yeah, maybe in ten years,' jokes Rob.

'Well, not really *together*,' says Caleb.

'What's that supposed to mean?' Taylah asks, turning towards him.

'You know what I mean,' Caleb says, 'we didn't choose it together both agreeing, you wanted it and I thought it was ridiculous – it is ridiculous. Nearly $40 for a plate! That's not even plate sized! It's tiny!'

'Well, we don't have to pick every single thing together.' Taylah says, turning towards the girls again, eyebrows raised. 'But everything in total will be things that are *ours* because *we* are together, your stuff and my stuff and the stuff we've both got is all together our stuff for our home.'

'Have you noticed lately,' Rob says, examining his bottle, 'that every bloody craft beer you could possibly buy is convict themed at the moment?'

Dylan reaches for his bottle. 'Never thought about it mate,' he says and takes a drink.

'Not always, just right now,' Rob adds.

Taylah rolls her eyes and Caleb turns his bottle over in his hands.

'This one is probably more pirate than convict,' Jess points out. 'Turquoise label and a black octopus?'

Katie laughs.

Rob shakes his head. 'Convicts did come in boats, but yeah, alright, maybe not this one so much, but convicts and pirates are not that different.' He takes a long drink from his bottle. 'Every other carton I nearly got definitely was. Guns and gum trees, iron masks. You name it.'

'Yeah I have seen some, now you mention it,' Dylan says.

Rob nods at him. 'There you go.'

'I'm sure we tried a Ned Kelly lager out the other weekend?' Caleb nods at Rob.

'You can buy that at the bottle-o, I saw it.'

'Do you mean convict or do you mean bushranger though?' Sarah asks.

'All the same,' Rob says.

'Not much of a difference, is there,' adds Dylan.

'Mascu-line Austra-lie,' Jess draws out in comic French.

'No women-in-bonnets beer though, is there,' Taylah says.

Rob laughs and rolls his eyes. 'Alright, sorry, I didn't realise the bloody women brigade was here. Bushranger-slash-Convict-Man-Beer is currently a popular theme that I noticed at the bottle shop this afternoon, when I was buying all of the booze you are now freely enjoying.'

'Cheers to that,' Dylan starts.

Sarah's phone rings in her pocket and she glances down to quickly see who it is. She steps out onto the small balcony to take the call. Jess excuses herself too for the bathroom and Katie gets up for the white wine in the fridge.

***

Dylan drains the last of his bottle and wipes his mouth on the back of his hand. He raises his eyebrows at Rob, leaving him and Caleb to their laughing piss-takes of the soft news that plays at 6 pm on weeknights, and stands to join Sarah on the balcony. She's still on the phone, leaning her head to the right as she talks, resting her elbows on the railing. He opens the glass sliding door just enough to poke his head out and catch some of the conversation. Sarah laughs into the phone and Dylan walks outside, closing the door again behind him. Taylah comes back from the bathroom and sits next to Caleb. She links her right arm through his left and reaches for her wine glass down the table. Katie smiles at her and glances outside. Sarah keeps talking, looking down the street. Dylan rests his back against the railing, arms crossed across his chest, his body facing inside but head turned towards Sarah. Rob stands to do a better impression of an alleged suburban disability pension cheater, trying to escape the show's journo and camera crew, running into the closed glass door of a gym. He does it again and again, each time his snapping head back in the thin air and further perfecting the dumbfounded frown. Caleb rests his head on his arms and laughs into the table. Taylah and Katie laugh too. They didn't hear the start of the conversation but anyone would know the impression. The video went viral last week.

'Do it again,' Jess laughs.

'Again, babe,' adds Katie.

Rob paces backwards, giving himself a greater run up. He starts walking with the frown but has to stop, laughing too hard. He bends over for a moment before composing himself. Shaking his arms, he fixes his face into the perfect frown and manages to hold it as he looks back at his friends around the table. He hurries in front of the lounge, shaking his head with angry confusion at the pretend camera crew behind him, and Dylan yells at Sarah outside. Rob runs into the imaginary glass door, snapping his head back again but sharper this time, turning to look out to the balcony. The others laugh but turn too, hearing the yell even over themselves. Dylan has his back to them but they can see Sarah, looking up to Dylan, her phone in her hand. The white light shines upwards into her face, illuminating the argument. She looks down into it and turns off the screen. Inside Rob half-laughs and sits down again next to Katie.

'Katie,' he says, and she turns her gaze away from the balcony. Rob frowns and gives the smallest shake of his head, telling her to stop staring.

The song changes in the bedroom. Caleb takes a long drink from his bottle. Jess and Taylah exchange looks. Dylan kisses Sarah's forehead outside and she slides her phone into her pocket, walking back in and smiling at the table as she passes them all for the bathroom. Dylan's shoulders rise slowly and drop again. He follows Sarah inside.

'What are youse laughing about then,' he smirks.

'Ah, just shit mate,' Rob says.

Dylan nods and walks to the fridge.

'How messed up is the plane, hey,' Jess says, breaking the heavy quiet. 'Two of them now. Two planes in one year from the same bloody airline. Jesus Christ.'

Caleb runs his hand through his hair. 'Yeah we were talking about it before. Three hundred people,' he says.

'Can't wrap my head around it,' says Jess. 'Not really.'

Katie stands and takes the two empty wine bottles from the table to the recycling bin. She sidesteps Dylan in the kitchen, avoiding his eyes, and gives the glass a quick rinse in the sink.

'How does it even,' Jess shakes her head.

'Something's wrong with them,' says Rob.

'What do you mean?' Jess says.

'There's something wrong with them.'

He emphasises *them* in a way they're too used to hearing. Them, those people, from over there, so strange and different, and worse than *us*.

'What do you...' Jess' slack hand knocks the top of her beer and the bottle falls to the ground. Dark glass shatters on the tiles. They scurry for paper towels to mop up the frothing fluid, shards balancing on their fingers. The discussion is dropped and the aircraft recedes from the room, forgotten again.

CHAPTER 8

The dirt road up to camp rose and fell with the hills as they cut inland away from the city. Three hired buses carried the three classes, six teachers, five volunteer mums and one volunteer dad, luggage, footballs, and bag of spare hats from lost property that forgetful kids have protested against wearing at Camp Lawson for fifteen or so years. They pulled slowly out of the school driveway early in the morning, past the parents waving them off, and pushed onto the highway that mirages in heat even in spring. The digital clock above the bus driver lit the two and a half hour drive. They all only really noticed it once, the minutes moving slowly with a faint electric tick, when they had to pull over for a spewer.

The buses had reached Camp Lawson around half-past ten in the morning, pulling up and unloading and shuffling kids between their allocated bunks just in time for lunch. The welcome brief by the camp staff and two hour long game of capture the flag, then bullrush, then stuck-in-the-mud and then free time and showers until the dinner bell rang was not enough to tire anyone. Hyped on the idea of being away from home, away from parents for two entire nights as one of ninety-two ten year olds sent the whole grade entirely mad. Shower-time was a relatively easy process. As wagered in the staff room last week, less than half of the grade actually bothered to wash. Taylah's only real duty was keeping watch in the girls' room, confiscating contraband such as spray deodorant and lip-gloss. Dinner was bolognese and broccoli, slopped onto plastic plates by the late-teenage camp staff. An after dinner game of spotlight was confined to the grassy middle of the main ground that the twelve cabins and two toilet blocks border around. Taylah and Morgan, the new sports teacher who Taylah was quickly becoming close friends with, volunteered to partner, in charge of herding out the deserters from behind the bunks and left-side block of loos. A group of girls tried to hide twice, falling over themselves and giggling whenever Taylah's torchlight sent them running back to the middle. There were enough trees and man-made timber obstacles that it took forty-five minutes for everyone to be found. The last survivor, a lanky kid from 5C, had climbed up a tree and wedged himself into a comfortable fork where he would have stayed all night if a lazy upwards swing of a torch hadn't caught his undone shoelace in the light.

Now, ten pm, stars pierce the black sky between bouts of dark cloud, and small eruptions of laughter from the bunks are slowly being outweighed by silence. The building ring is in darkness, bar faint lights from the toilets and the glowing mess hall where the moths swarm and teachers have retreated with bourbon and coke. Taylah accepts a heavy handed top up as the bottle makes its way around the table. A phone buzzes among them. Torchlight flashes across the grass. Seven bunkers shush an eighth and the cicadas keeping delivering, the night choir cloaking the whispers and a sprinting, close-mouthed first kiss.

***

The cicadas seem quieter in the morning, but it's only in comparison to the roar of breakfast. Honey and maple syrup sticky every surface. Pancakes are rolled, sliced, and stuffed whole into faces. Fingers are wiped on clean t-shirts.

Mr Grange, the most senior of the three sports teachers on camp duty, stands at a fold out table at the head of the room and blows the silver whistle hanging around his neck.

'Good morning campers!'

'Good mor-ning Mis-ter Grange,' they sing back.

A near empty bottle of syrup squirts out a wet fart down the back and he's lost them to laughter already. He gives it a second, pushing down his own smirk, then the whistle blows again. A room of red faces turn up.

'Rightio. We've got a full schedule today everyone so I need your eyes and ears up here. Today's activities include low ropes, kayaking, bush walking, the orienteering puzzle and an obstacle course. You've been divided into five groups and groups will rotate through each activity. The group lists are on five different posters around this room.'

Grange points to the five teachers with the different coloured lists spaced out around the edges.

'Your first job is to find your name on a list. There will be one teacher, one parent and one camp leader per group. They will tell you which activity you are starting with. You must stay with this group all day. We will do two activities, then have morning tea, then two more activities, lunch, one more activity, and then you will practice your act for tonight's talent show. Your activity group is also your talent show group. Is that clear?'

Every students nods, full attention given for the first time all year, and before the whispers creep in about who's in what group, Mr Grange continues.

'Right. It's 8:40. You have exactly twenty minutes,' he pauses as the kids' legs itch to run, drawing out the instructions so they all know what they're rushing for, 'to stack your plates in the wash tubs near the door, brush your teeth, put some sunscreen on, and be back here *in your groups*. It might take five minutes to find your name on the right list so make sure you're back here quick-smart.'

Grange holds up a single finger and the kids wait for the green light.

'Okay?'
The room nods.
'I can't hear you.'
'Yes Mis-ter Grange.'
'Good.' He nods.
They stare.
The silence peaks.
'Go.'

***

Taylah's group are called The Magpies. She has nineteen kids, a handful from her normal class at school but most of them not. Their camp leader is Nicole, a blonde nineteen year old who graduated from high school last year. When the grade returns, wiping toothpaste from around their mouths before it dries into a white slick, Nicole and Taylah check the names off their group list twice, top down then bottom up, making sure no one's switched names for a day or confused themselves accidentally. They're on the obstacles first and then have a bushwalk before morning tea that covers the local fauna and flora, then low ropes and kayaking and lunch. Throughout the morning Taylah slides into background management with Joanne, their volunteer mum, and lets Nicole take the lead. It suits the class fine. The kids, only needing to make eye contact with Taylah to know to get on with it, test Nicole instead. They can tell she's not as old as their school staff, and also not a real teacher, but she isn't exactly a kid. Listening when they have to, answering back when they can, the kids mostly turn out their model behaviour when they realise they don't need to know any answers or compete for a star to stick on the classroom wall.

***

The lake is a five minute downhill bush bash from the cabins. Short ferns lean over the sandy path, only worn wide enough for one person at a time. The skinny green fingers brush their bare legs as they traipse towards the water. Every few steps someone holds still, scratching where the fern or bug or rock or fly has itched their calf. Taylah brings up the rear, stomping her feet and hoping the kids in front of her are enough to ward off snakes. The bush moves constantly, touched by a breeze that sways the tall gums and snakes its way through the low ferns carpeting everything. One of the girls screams at a rustle on her right, and her friend screams too in reply. They run past the boys in front. Nicole doesn't bother to turn around.

'They're more scared of you than you are of them. Let's keep moving.'

The sand underneath them thins right out and the bush gives up a few feet before the water. Yellow kayaks lay at the water's edge, surrounded by small footprints, still wet from the last group. A lizard abandons its exploration of the sopping pile of faded life jackets and scurries back into the growth. Nicole lifts one of the paddles. The Magpies grab a partner before she has to say any more.

Taylah pairs herself with Chase, a kid she thinks is a rotter, rather than leaving him with Joanne. He was too busy fiddling with a rubber band looped around his finger to notice the others pulling together in pairs. He feels Taylah looking down at him and he stares back up at her. Nicole claps her hands together. It's time to get in.

The lake isn't the dark blue you'd normally expect of this much fresh water, but a soft brown, the same colour and gradient as gummy coke bottles. At the sandy edge the lake water is clear. The colour creeps in as it gets deeper, down to its dark brown middle.

Once they're in and not wobbling quite as much, Nicole leads them out onto deeper water. They circle round to the right, anti-clockwise, like long yellow ducks on the dark surface. Nicole points out features around the edge that she's learnt and rehearsed over the past few weeks – a bird's nest balanced between two leafless branches, the peak of a distant mountain further west, a patch of blackened trees where a bushfire ripped through and the stark strip of white trunked gums where the blaze was quickly contained. A white plane passes high overhead. Their faces draw up at the distant metal grumble, necks stretching back, blinking into the sun.

Two kayaks race forwards and then float almost to the back of the yellow pack, before racing again to the tip of Nicole's boat in the lead. Taylah gave them a warning look the first time, feeling that she should, but decides to let it go. Nicole double checked their life jackets earlier and competent swimming's been a compulsory part of the curriculum since they all started school aged five.

Each time the winning two of the four girls cheer, lifting their paddles from the water and pumping the air. On the third race, as the pack passes the white pole that marks the turn-back point, the back two racers paddle furiously to take the lead. They pull through the water, propelling over the choppy brown surface. They take a gamble and cut between two other boats, non-racers, managing to splash two boys and nearly capsize another duo in the process. Wet shrieks ring out and the race erupts. Five boats in the middle push forwards, knocking paddle to plastic, helping most of the water find its way into the air.

Nicole, a few lengths out in front, taking the sudden noise for steady enthusiasm, signals for the group to swing left and slowly cut back across deeper water. She glances back to check everyone can actually turn. The five boats scream towards her. She blows her whistle and paddles faster herself, creating a touch more distance before turning sideways across them, marking an end to the race more than a finish line. Taylah watches Chase, sitting in front of her in the boat. His paddle hovers above the water for a moment, hesitating. He wants to tear off with the rest of them. He turns his head slightly towards her, the tiniest of turns, a listening reflex more than a move. Taylah keeps paddling the same, keeping her time, having to stop herself from yelling out across the lake. It wouldn't make any difference at this point. She leaves the on-water peacekeeping to Nicole and her whistle.

Seeing the collision coming, four of the racing boats stop their paddles, plunging them into the water to slow their speed. The girls who started the ruckus, now the two girls in the lead, are the last to realise. They are laughing and looking about when the others see Nicole cut across them. For two long seconds they paddle on. Nicole could out race them, easily, having eight years in life and six weeks of camp experience on them. But Nicole stays still. The girls realise and do everything but abandon ship. The other four boats pull up together. Taylah cruises in with Chase and the other non-racing groups. The girls, in the lead, slow to a floating creep across the brown lake. Nicole eyeballs them. She isn't going to move. The girls push their paddles deeper down. They slow. And slow. And nearly stop. A metre between the boats. Half a metre. Nicole raises her whistle to her lips. Five centimetres. The girls flinch. Two.

The girls' kayak kisses the side of Nicole's. In first place. They stare up at her. Nicole stares back. Whistle between lips. Air still. Taylah goes to speak but the silence is broken before her. A kookaburra laughs on the banks. Its sharp call echoes out between them, the nine plastic yellow ducks on the lake. A second bird joins in and then it's Nicole, dropping the whistle for a laugh. Taylah laughs as well, and the kids look back at her, searching for permission. Chase giggles in front, and she doesn't scold him, and all of the others fall apart too. The kookaburra flies off into the scrub. Nicole shakes her head and leads them all back to the shore.

***

Wet up to the knees and with damp patches everywhere else, The Magpies single file back up the sandy path to lunch. Two girls hang back behind the others, non-racing paddlers, whispering close beside the beached kayaks. They jump when Taylah walks back towards them, not seeing the teacher until she was almost in range of their conversation.

'Come on girls, what's happening?' Taylah motions for them to follow the others up the path. 'It's lunch time, let's go.'

They nod together. The shorter of the pair, a girl with blonde hair pulled back into a ponytail looks down at her wet white sneakers. One hand tugs at her sleeve of her t-shirt. She doesn't look up again. Taylah turns to the other girl she knows, Ruby, who's a head taller than the blonde. Her long black hair is still in the two braids her mother did yesterday morning. Ruby starts to say something but her friend cuts her a quick look. She looks down at her shoes too and starts to walk, letting her friend hurry to be in front.

As the bush starts to take over from the sand again, Taylah gives one last look over her shoulder to make sure no one's left behind. Chase is up ahead with Nicole and so are the two gold medallists of the kayak crash, giggling behind her, asking questions about boys and shaving her legs now that she's cool and didn't rouse on them, even though they broke her no-splashing and her no-running-into-anyone rules. Ruby and her friend have stopped again and are arguing a few feet into the scrub. Taylah walks into the end of their argument.

'It's okay,' Ruby says.

Her friend clutches at her arm, frowning and begging her not to.

'What else are we gonna do Soph?' Ruby shakes her off and turns to Taylah.

'Miss Brown,' she says, glancing back at the other girl for quick forgiveness. 'Can you please help us?'

Taylah nods and looks up ahead, seeing how far the others have got. 'What's up?'

'It's just,' Ruby starts. 'Sophie just has, well, she's just got,' she nods her head like that's all it needs.

Taylah waits for more explanation.

'See, we came down here after low ropes and she's not been feeling well and now in the kayak's she's, and we don't have – we had to wait because I saw and I told her, and so we weren't *not* doing what you said, we were just…'

Ruby looks to Sophie and Sophie hunches her shoulders up to her ears. She squeezes her fist tighter around her pink t-shirt sleeve and bursts into tears.

'I'm sorry Sophie, it's okay, it's okay Soph,' Ruby coos and hugs her friend.

Sophie cries harder and Taylah crouches down in the sand.

'What is it Sophie?' Taylah asks. 'What's happened?'

Two boys ahead on the path stop and turn around to see what the noise is. Taylah nods at them to keep walking and they do, wanting lunch more than to know what the tears are about.

Ruby pats Sophie's head and leans towards Taylah. 'Miss,' she whispers. 'She's got her period.'

Taylah frowns in sympathy. She nods and pauses for a moment, mind flashing back to her own first morning at thirteen and the dark blood on her white sheets, the white toilet paper, the gut punch pain and redbrown clots and plastic rustling in the school toilets that gives the game away.

'Right,' Taylah says, noticing for the first time Sophie's cream coloured cargo pants.

Sophie turns her head to look at Taylah. Her fringe has matted to her face. There's Ruby with her braids, patting her best friend's blonde head, and Taylah with her knees in the sand, a crying ten year old girl in front of them, cream pants sopping with lake water and a few drops of thick blood, pushed into puberty on her first school camp with ninety other kids to walk past at lunch, and no parent to hug or squirm away from.

'Congratulations Sophie,' Taylah tries, straight faced. 'Welcome to the club. This is a wonderful step up in your life but also, I won't lie, a pretty shitty thing.' She smiles and Sophie giggles at the swearing. Taylah gives her a quick hug and outlines the game plan. 'You're a bit sunburnt Soph, so crying isn't making your face any more red. Don't worry about it. If people ask why you're late at lunch you can tell them that you just went to the toilet and it won't be a lie so you can say it with a straight face.'

Both girls half smile.

'Right, Rube. Walk Soph to the loos closest here so you don't have to walk past everyone at lunch. You can walk behind her if you want but honestly, if you're quick, everyone's at lunch so no one's gonna see you anyway. We're gonna take care of you, Sophie. Alright?'

Sophie nods and wipes her wet face.

'Good. Ruby, find Sophie some clean knickers and pants. Maybe a shirt too cause you can get out of your wet lake clothes anyway before they smell. I'll go find a pad or something. Is your stomach sore? We have Panadol somewhere. When you're changed just run cold water over any blood stains and maybe a bit of hand soap if you need. Should come out no problem.'

With a final squeeze the three head back up the clearing. They part at the edge of the buildings, nodding silently to one another, the two girls heading for the bathrooms and Taylah for the staff room where the first aid kit is kept. She sidesteps a boy outside sitting on the grass itching at bites on his legs and nearly runs into Nicole coming out of the building with a fistful of Band-Aids.

'Boys, I tell you,' Nicole laughs on the way past. 'You alright?'

Taylah nods. 'Shark week supplies?'

'Ah, there's always one. Cupboard on the right.'

Taylah thanks her and finds the stash, a tray of rainbow coloured boxes between the spare loo rolls. She opts for pads, finding the heavy ones with wings and picking up a thick handful, resenting the memory of the nappy feel but knowing camp might not be the nicest time for a ten year old to test out tampons. Doubling back for a strip of paracetamol and plastic cup of water, Morgan catches up with her, having finished lunch.

'Hey, Tay,' she calls out.

Taylah slows so she can catch her.

'Whatcha doin? Your ass is a bit wet.' She grins. 'I didn't see you at lunch.'

'Yeah, I'll get there eventually.' Taylah nods to the bright plastic in her hands. 'What a shitty place to get your period. Ten is so young.'

Morgan grimaces. 'Ugh. Thank god we don't ever have to be teenagers again.' She exaggerates a full body squirm and grins. 'And thank god it's you and not me,' she nods at the pads in Taylah's hand.

Taylah frowns. 'Thank god indeed.'

Ruby runs between the trees in front of them, her arms full of Sophie's clean clothes, in a new outfit herself, a stroke of best friend brilliance.

***

Lunch is triangle cut sandwiches, fruit juice and oranges. Crusts go in the bin with the rinds, ready to be poured on the compost. Kids in the middle of the hall take turns blowing up and jumping on their empty juice cartons. Ruby and Sophie sit together at a table with some other friends. They smile at Taylah once and turn back to their sandwiches.

***

The orienteering puzzle heads in a different direction to their morning bushwalk. Forcibly divvied into groups of four or three, The Magpies have to use a clue sheet, a hand-drawn map and compass to find different letters hidden in the close scrub. They'll bring them all together to make one word. Nicole and Taylah perch on rocks at the top of a slope and the kids pour down the hill with Joanne to where the letters are, turning over rocks and looking up.

'You thought this out well,' Taylah tells Nicole as the first lot find a letter W, sticky taped to the back of a tree. 'We can just let them loose but still see every one of them from up here.'

Nicole taps her nose. 'Isn't it.'

Taylah gives two thumbs up to three girls who scream "I" up the hill.

'Now if any of them go down we'll know exactly where.' Nicole points out a rough square in trees. 'Rarely a snake in this spot. Spiders at worst. But we scour it in the breaks when we stick the letters back up.'

The Magpies rustle between the trees, crawling or stopping every few steps to hunch over a map. Chase slaps a paperbark trunk with a skinny fern leaf he's plucked from the ground. Three other boys run down the right hand boundary. Nicole yells at them when they've gone too far, motioning for them to come back.

'Better give 'em a hand,' she nods to Taylah and takes off down the hill chanting, 'You can do it! Who's gonna win? Which team is the best?'

Taylah picks a stick up and traces it through the dirt. Brown dust coats her palms and collects under her unpainted fingernails. There's less yelling for a moment, less running through the trees as the kids swarm around Nicole for some help. Taylah can't hear them properly. They're too far down the hill. There's only the general clatter children make and birds sweeping the trees. Rustles in the grass. Yellow bottomed ants at her feet. She watches their pushing and their patience. The kids from her own class changing around the others. Smiling, laughing, scooting off when a clue has been delivered.

The sun sinks lower behind the trees and when they're done The Magpies canter up the hill, nine separate letters in tow spelling the word *Wiradjuri*. Nicole winds out a story about local Indigenous customs and possum-skin cloaks that's just long enough to last the walk back to the food hall, just enough to tick a box on the camp's educational-experiences-inclusive-of-cultural-heritage checklist.

***

The talent show is a riot. Eighty percent of it is girls getting out nothing more than fits of contagious laughter, and fifteen percent boys standing shoulder to shoulder at the back of the stage purposefully forgetting dance moves. One group, The Wombats, share a mumbled acrostic poem, C-A-M-P L-A-W-S-O-N, faces down. Taylah and Nicole's group request that the lights are turned off, telling a scary story under torchlight that starts at a camp, just like this one, about children disappearing and ends with Chase grabbing Mrs Davis' legs under her chair, ninety children screaming as one in the dark.

The last group run a skit about, as they loosely introduce, Australia. Fourteen of the fifteen potter about the stage miming a sausage sizzle, thin white bread arms of one kid wrapped around another who wriggles like a burning rocket, a small herd of sheep bleating on all fours, a cantering bushman who's top half cracks a whip and the bottom clops along like a horse, and a lifeguard saving people at the beach. One kid, full of cheek, wears a blue singlet (the kind that's somehow still called a wife-beater) complete with pillow-stuffed beer belly and black rubber thongs on his feet. He staggers around the front of the hall holding a can of coke, a beer can stand-in that he still would have had to beg one of the camp staff for. The corks hanging off his brown hat knock into one other. He does nothing but swat at mostly unreal bugs, skol the empty can with his head back and pretend to fart, lifting one leg, fanning the air behind his backside. The act is so slick it's like watching a dog swim out of the deep end of the pool for the first time. An act grown in his bones.

Mr Grange loses it. He slaps his knee and wipes his eyes, hooting louder than the rest of the grade combined.

'Darl,' the boy says when he realises his pull. 'You've gone and burnt the snags.' He points at a sheep and the audience roars. 'Aw, tell him he's dreaming.'

The group finish with a hand-on-heart delivery of four Peter Allen song lines they know from a Qantas ad that aired before they were born, closing their eyes for *New York to Rio and old London town*, despite few of them having folks who can afford overseas holidays, and with *no matter how far or how wide I roam*, the whole full room double belts the final line, screaming the pitch out the second time. *I still call Australia home. I still call Australia home.*

***

Eleven-thirty and the bunks black out. Moths crowd in the hall again. Coke tonight, with a choice of bourbon or rum. Mrs Davis pulls out a block of Cadbury Fruit and Nut she's saved for the last night.

'I knew we'd need it,' she laughs, breaking four squares off and sliding the purple plastic wrapper down the table.

CHAPTER 9

Caleb finally gets the words out. 'How long's it gonna be for, Tay?'

She shrugs. 'I don't know, babe. However long he likes, he's my brother.' She pulls away and crosses to the kitchen.

Neighbours chatter down the hallway. The elevator dings.

'However long he needs.'

'I'm just asking.'

'Yeah I know you are. But I can't just...'

'I'm not asking you to kick him out Monday.' Caleb holds his palms up, shaking his head. 'I want him here just as much as you do, alright. I already said it's fine for him to stay.'

Taylah looks to the bathroom door, hoping Brett can't hear them over the shower. Brett's unpacked duffel bag and bed sheet, hanging half off the lounge he's a foot too long for, only take up a hundredth of their space but three nights on the couch are already making the company feel like a crowd. The coffee table in the wrong spot. TV running on mute. Phone buzzing incessantly at night. Caleb eating cereal at the kitchen bench with the curtains still closed because Brett's sleep only comes with the sunrise. Ashtray sticking out like a sore thumb in a non-smoking apartment, growing mountains of black dust overnight that are washed away again each afternoon.

Taylah drops her voice. 'It won't be that long, okay. If it's too much we can just say, and he might go back up to Mum and Dad's for a while.'

Caleb exhales and walks over to hug her again, pulling her head into his chest. She resists it for a moment, then wraps her arms around his waist. He kisses her head and brushes her hair back off her shoulders, patting it down the way she complains about but he likes doing, appreciating the blonde softness, forgiving the loose strands that get lost in everything and the not-quite-empty bottles of product that multiply under the bathroom sink.

Caleb pushes his words out again, squeezing Taylah tight. 'I could take him to look at apartments?'

She pushes him off. 'For Christ's sake, Caleb. Give it at least a week, will you? Can you do that? He's not being bloody lazy okay. He needs help.'

'I am trying to help. Sitting here doing nothing won't do him any good. He has to get out and try. He needs to help himself.'

The shower stops and Taylah turns to the coffee machine. Caleb balls his fist and pushes it, lightly, into the bench.

'I have to go,' he says.

'See ya.'

'Don't…'

'Don't what?' Taylah turns and snaps back.

'Come on.'

The bathroom window slides open, breaking their sudden silence.

Taylah holds her breath and waits for the door.

In the bathroom, Brett wipes the steam clouded mirror and pulls his blue t-shirt and shorts on, skin still slightly damp. He rubs his red eyes. He can hear them. He throws his towel over the rail and stays to brush his teeth.

Hearing the tap run, Taylah slides her coffee cup under the machine. It whirrs and dribbles out a hot black shot. Caleb lifts his fist off the bench. He checks the time. Six minutes until the train. His shoulders sink and he looks to the sun outside.

'Milk?' Taylah offers.

'Yeah, please.'

***

She drives him to the station, two trains later than his usual one but neither of them unforgivably late, each morning for the rest of the week. A new ritual. The three minutes together in the car offer some room to breathe.

In the loading zone outside the station Taylah puts the car into park. Caleb picks up his bag from between his feet. She looks at him, his dark hair, brown watch, hastily ironed blue shirt. Green eyes. He rests a hand on her shoulder and leans in to kiss her goodbye. Yes, she thinks. Okay. This is the man and this is the view, the scene, this face, these lips on my cheek. The way those hands pat his pants, checking for essentials in the front pockets before he pulls himself out of the car. The way he smiles with his eyebrows lifting. He at work and me at work and the back seat empty, for now, no tiny sticky fingers – yes even to the fighting. Yes to the heavy air when he doesn't say what he should or does say what he shouldn't, but that's always temporary and maybe this isn't. Caleb isn't. The two of us aren't, she thinks, and they could just keep doing this forever. And maybe this is happy, in the middle.

Caleb leans back in to kiss her again, properly, squeezing her hand.

Yes, she thinks. Okay.

***

When Brett's been with them a week they facetime their parents, like Taylah normally does on a Tuesday. Caleb opens a pack of beef in the kitchen, cooking a stir-fry and rice, staying in the background of the call and chiming in when needed.

'Good, good,' Liz says again and calls her husband to the phone. 'David, the kids are on. Yes, now.'

The wait for him to press save and plod down the hall from the office, Taylah checking dinner in the meantime.

'Hi guys,' their dad projects, waving at the screen.

'Hi Dad,' Taylah waves back.

'No need to yell,' Brett frowns. 'We're just here.'

'You're not though are you,' Liz points out.

'How's it going, then?' David nods. He sips his beer and crosses his arms behind Liz.

Taylah does most of the talking. Brett smiles and agrees and says everything's good, everything's fine, his boss is alright and he'll go back to work soon, and he rang up about two apartments this morning.

'Sounds like you're fair shot of him, mate.' David finishes and leaves the screen to put his bottle in the recycling.

'It wasn't him, Dad,' Brett sighs and wipes his face hard, pulling at a headache under his skin.

'How's work, ma,' Taylah interjects.

Liz smiles the way mums do, pulling a perfect face out of some inside place. She spoons out enough story to move the call along past Brett's break up. Her day of ordering new books and planning a summer reading group for the local kids, figuring out how to best tell parents about it over the internet. The morning tea they threw yesterday for Dot's birthday, a woman who volunteers at the library and has lived in Mareebra for sixty-odd years. Ginger cake. Coconut covered biscuits. Remembering not to put the milk in before the tea, God help them all. Liz vacuuming between the aisles of books when everyone else has gone, humming to herself among the dust. Brett nods more and more as he itches for a smoke or a drink, both, just some quiet with his pressing thoughts and no talking, no answers to rack his brain for.

Liz texts her daughter afterwards, asking what she really wanted to and telling her to keep her updated. What he's really like, how he's really doing. Taylah responds quickly, standing in the kitchen as Brett and Caleb watch whatever's on TV. How he's taking a break from work for the week and that his boss is surprisingly understanding for a big bloke who coordinates logistics. That it's a good sign Brett could even ask for that much. She tells her mother it'll be fine, starting to learn the smile and the right lines.

***

Taylah catches him later, awake. TV quietly playing a cartoon. Her brother holding a joint out the window as she tiptoes into the kitchen for a glass of water. Brett jumps when he sees her but doesn't put anything out. She nods, and he nods, she fills a tall glass and he looks back out the window again.

***

Taylah checks his texts just once, jumping on the phone when Brett leaves it to charge as he goes out for a walk. Looking for a clue from his ex or some comfort from a friend, or good news from a boss. She can't unlock it, not knowing the passcode, but can read the first few lines on the screen when they buzz in. It's spam. Nothing. A text from the phone provider. Caleb raises his eyebrows.

'Just ask him.'

She doesn't bother checking again.

***

There's the smoke again, a few nights. Taylah knows now and seeks it out, sensitive to the smell floating out and in their windows. On Thursday she beats Caleb home and knocks twice on the bathroom door, the first time thinking Brett's ignoring her or shaving his face so he doesn't speak, and the second realising the quiet and the phone buzzing and no splashes meaning no wet razor. When she bangs again and calls out, with a break in her voice, Brett calls back.

'Stop. I'm just sitting,' he says, and he was.

'You want some water?' Taylah pushes for an excuse.

The door unlocks after a shuffle and his quiet face is fine. His pale face. Sitting on the floor of the small room, the cold tiles, little window. Pulling it together again.

***

Jess and Jessie come around on the weekend as the sun goes down, bringing bags of takeaway Vietnamese. The five pile onto the lounge and pull up chairs in front of the TV with their bowls full, Brett's belongings away in Taylah and Caleb's room. Jessie passes around the prawn rolls and laughs at her girlfriend's jokes, touching her arm and pushing her hair back with the electric waves you always crave at the start of things. New Jess mimics girls on the train they sat behind on their way over tonight, frowning and flipping her hair: *I'm the most liberal – no, not like political, I'm the most open-minded person I know. I think about the refugees, like, all the time.* Brett flicks through the channels, dripping noodle soup down the front of his blue t-shirt. He sucks it off the cotton and new Jess groans. Brett nearly chokes, laughing at the fact Taylah hardly gets through a meal without needing to do the same. *Harry Potter*'s started playing. They don't need to verbally agree to watch it. You'd never say no. Caleb says he's got it somewhere on DVD but it's on now so they sit through the ads anyway. Taylah fetches everyone glasses of water. It's warm and rice drops onto the carpet, soup is slurped, lemongrass runs on the breeze, and the night rolls on easy. The film ends and the girls leave and they all sleep.

***

With four weeks left of work until the long school holidays start mid-December, Taylah ramps up her approach. Small certificates. Kids racing home with stickers on their chests, proudly being the best. Nervous about the next year, with no contract signed yet, Taylah's thoughts oscillate each day between strategically reaching the next step of the career ladder and trying to apply logic to the timing of having kids. Caleb isn't there yet himself, with her or with work, so it's not something she's game to bring up yet. Moved by the need for money and the next chapter it's nearly time for, she puts more thought and humour into everything she can, even down to their weekly spelling test.

'Humidity,' she calls out as the paces the front of the classroom. 'In the strange state of Queensland, north of here, where the crocodiles live and bananas grow, there is a lot of humidity. Humidity.'

Positive feedback from parents can make a real difference to the game at this point. A word offered to the Principal as he does the smiling rounds at the Christmas parade. A few sentences via email. All of it building to a quiet office meeting that, hopefully, ends in a contract offer handshake. The next chapter. Now Taylah, and every other twenty-something with a fresh enough degree sitting in a drawer or hanging on their parents' wall, sprint to the finish line as the weeks heat up. Killing kids with kindness for even a scrap of light for the end of their short-term tunnels, a reference or an "I know someone at," being seen as the right kind of teacher, just enough to swim through the summer holidays.

'Nectarine,' she presses on, spoon-feeding them the syllables. 'Nec-ta-rine.'

***

Taylah and Brett decide to spend their Sunday together at Manly, a picture perfect beach on the lavish north, two among thousands on the bluebird sunny Sunday. The main drag running along the beach heaves on days like this. Before the crack of dawn exercisers sprint sand laps, then lycra-clad brunch buyers squeeze lemon and cracked pepper onto their organic avocado toast and pat their pockets for the coins they know they don't carry when they pass the strip's rough sleepers. Over lunchtime it fills with families of sun-screened beach goers and oiled up sun soakers, the briefly lost kids, screaming swimmers ripping off the bluebottles and finding thick welts under the sting, and the afternoon squeezes out walking tourists with their white socks before the exercisers-turned-drinkers roll in again. Day trippers from overseas, interstate, and the other side of the city flocking with the cashed up locals to the beach. Lifeguards controlling the beat.

The old green and cream boat is surprisingly busy on their early trip over, more so it seems than normal hot Sundays. Taylah and her brother snag a spot standing at the back of the ferry leaning against the green rail where they can look back into the harbour. People pile in after them. Young parents with flatbed prams and babies shaking noisy toys, grandparents being wheeled out on the same trip they used to be in charge of, tourists sweating through their sunscreen. Brett and Taylah both look down over the railing. The depth of the Harbour is always surprising no matter how many times you come. When their folks brought them down to the Quay as kids, walking them round from the Bridge to the Opera House and back again, they'd hop over the tiny floor signs at the east end that mark the old shoreline. The difference between 1889, 1902 and 1935 tides cemented into the path, minute compared to the width of country, radical considering the apparent permanence of the concrete harbour. Bronze reminders of the quick changing times for anyone who can tear their eyes from the towering view.

When the boat takes off, two teen boys next to them huddle around a phone and look up to discuss the cricket scores with their father every few minutes. They nod at each other and harp on like the seagulls springing around up above. The boat putts around the white opera sails, past the tiny old military post that's recently been a fine-dining island, and everyone at the back of the ferry looks to the bridge and upstream into the country. A sleek black and silver boat shoots past, cutting through the waves like a knife through a bed sheet.

***

Taylah checks her phone, accidentally clicking into her notes app instead of the camera. Before she can swipe out of it the fake paper loads and there's a list there, a few half-sentences about living and lounge rooms, on collapsing two lives and wanting to care less than she's expected to. She reads through it. Remembering her good bad change of things. The gaping hole of questions she maybe should have asked herself about what you want versus need and how to furnish a house so that brothers can drop by for weeks unexpectedly. The resolution comes back around to her now that there's something obvious to think about. She glances up at Brett. He leans over the railing, eyes closed into the sun. Taylah opens a new page and writes again. Types again. Angling the screen slightly away from her brother. What's good, what's bad, what can change. Everything can, she thinks.

> *Good:*
> *Now that things are shit you can see how good*
> *everything else is*
> *normally*
>
> *Bad:*
> *Even if we try to make it seem not too bad, Brett is bad,*
> *this isn't good*
> *He's unwell*
> *And thank Christ Mum and Dad have the money to*
> *lend him for rent, breaking the lease, for the doctor and*
> *whatever else the doctor brings*

Taylah turns the change on herself, looking up from her screen to see the blue churning out behind the boat and thinking *what on earth can I do*.

They pull further out of the Harbour, zooming out from the city, and frustration bubbles up inside her – a moment of clarity, or something close to it, as the buildings recede and she can see the skyline in a single frame rather than how she usually sees it, all around her, from inside.

Change waits, the cursor flashing over the blank space on her screen.

Taylah takes a photo of the view from the back of the boat. The sun sparks on the choppy water. Blue sky. Blue sea. Brett's hand on the green railing at the bottom. A short strand of her blonde hair whipping into the frame.

For what more is there in this place than days like this, with the sun on your skin and the water, the way the air smells, the unique flickering heat. The sandy dirt. The soft green of the gum trees.

The boat makes a turn to the left and slows, ready to pull into the shelter of the headland.

***

'I just didn't think it was that serious.' Brett scuffs his shoe on the path and they pause at the top of the concrete beach stairs.

Seagulls cry to each other overhead. A girl rinses off under the open shower next to them and they step to the side, out of the way of a large passing family complete with two umbrellas and watermelon-painted blow up ball. Wind blows through the trees.

'And it's not like it's that easy to talk about. Isn't that literally the point – anxiety makes me anxious, right? You can't just call people up and be all like, "hello, I'm an anxious wreck of a human and everything's gone to shit and I can't get out of bed, send help." And you're busy here with Caleb, and Mum and Dad are settled into it without us up there and I just didn't want to…'

'I'm always here, Brett. Always. Just pick up the phone or, I dunno.' Taylah sighs. 'I'm your sister.'

'Yeah, I know kid. I know.'

The both look out to the water, the far off end to the blue.

'I am gonna go, there's this group therapy the doctor referred me to.'

'Yeah?'

'Mum said they'd pay, so.'

Taylah nods out at the ocean, knowing because she and her mum have talked about it all already but letting him speak.

'And I will, okay. Let you in, or whatever bullshit it is that people say.' He nods. 'I'll try.'

Taylah wraps an arm around his neck, dropping her head onto his tall shoulder.

***

There's a clear rip in the water. A clean patch without whitewash that tempts those who don't know right in, flies to the sweet scent, nerves into the calm-looking slice of blue. Two lifeguards have set up in front of it on their buggy, parked near the unread signs, the beach busy enough for personal prevention. Umbrellas and beach tents dot the sand. Over every other white inch sprawl pink towels, green towels, blue and white flag towels the shop up the street sells for three times as much as you should pay. Bare skin soaking in the sun. Babies pat the wet shoreline where the warm water kisses their tiny feet. Dads dig great holes in the sand, pushing together palaces and teaching their kids to drip wet sandy turrets through their fingers. Boogie boards stick on the sand after a screaming ride. Pink zinc slicks faces like war paint. Old tanned couples walk up and down the strip like elephants who don't need any bronze-cemented reminders of the changing tide. Swimmers pack the best place, just after the break where there's only water under your feet and you can lie, nose to the sky, floating up and over.

They pick a spot to the right of the flags, flicking their towels out and stripping off. Taylah tucks her purse under her shirt and Brett does the same with his keys. They walk down towards the water, looking around, not stopping when they get to the edge. The first wave is cool and they turn when the sets hit, letting the water smack into their sides until they've walked too close to the breaking point and have to dive under without hesitating. The wave rumbles overhead. The water is easy to swim through. Coming up on the other side Taylah slicks her hair back and Brett flicks the water from his in her direction. She splashes him and they grin, diving under the next wave just in time. The sets roll in quickly but the waves die right off between, the horizon running flat far off in front of them. They paddle out further than they can touch. Brett holds his breath and drops under, seeing how far down the bottom is. He's not down for long.

'You can feel the pull,' Taylah says as he comes back up.

'What?' Brett unplugs the water from his ears.

'Bit of a drag.'

'Yeah. We're not far out though.' He turns back to the beach, checking if they've drifted from the middle of the flags. The two red and yellow beacons wrinkle in the wind. They're in the okay zone. Another wave comes up behind them and they sail over it, Brett with his toes towards the beach.

Two boys paddle past on their boogie boards, taking a break from screaming into shore, bellies to the wave. Finding an open-enough space they climb onto their boards, wriggling forwards until they're steady enough to both sit with their legs over each side. They float together. Drag their fingers through the water. Paddle. Point out fish. Slowly egg-beat their legs and hold the front of the board tight with their hands when a rolling wave comes.

'We used to do that. D'you remember?'

'Yeah,' Brett says. 'I had the sickest board. With the shark bite painted on the front corner.'

'I remember.'

A large wave rolls in in the distance, swelling higher than all the rest. The water beneath them runs towards it. Dragging the swimmers out deeper. Taylah reaches for the sand with her toes. Her foot sinks into nothing. Just more sea. Water splashes into her nose. Salt burn. Her heart jumps. A quick kick of panic. A sharp breath. A drop inside her stomach. She looks around, back to the beach, over to Brett. He's swimming out with the drag, knowing not to pull against the tide. Taylah pulls herself after him. The opposite way she wants to go. She kicks harder and her mind flicks to the endless deep. The nothing under her feet. Blue. Shark. Drowning. Black.

The wave passes, with a bit more pull than the last, not paying them any attention. They float over it. People behind them scream, whoop, laugh, having survived the dumping break. Taylah breathes out again. They float for a while longer, melting into the surface of the sea, then sidestroke back across the beach when they realise they're out of the flags. The sun beats down on their faces, drying the salt on their lips.

'God, I haven't been swimming for so long. Not in the surf.' Brett rolls onto his back, lazily, then pushes himself over into a slow underwater backflip. He comes up again with a mouthful of water and spurts it into the sky. 'Not since Sam.'

***

They body surf back into the beach once their faces don't just feel hot but are red, already, which means tomorrow the burn will be bad. Taylah holds her bikini bottoms up as the whitewash crashes behind them. A girl scoots past her on an orange foam board, her dad cheering her on behind. Brett sidesteps a family throwing a beach footy across the waves and nearly runs into another young couple. Both early teens, they stand still with their arms wrapped around each other as the water smacks into their shins. Not noticing anything but the other's bare skin. Taylah and Brett both smirk as they pass them.

'That's not what I was doing at thirteen.' Brett shakes his head.

'Aw, what about Casey M?' Taylah teases.

He laughs and kicks the shallow water at Taylah. 'Casey bloody M. We did hold hands one lunch time, you know. Shared a pizza rounda or two.'

'I know,' Taylah laughs. 'I was spying on you with Brittany.'

Brett gasps. 'You would too, you little perves.' They laugh and he chases her up the beach.

***

Back at their towels they agree to head off for an ice cream. Taylah dries off her hair and it scrunches up, curling full of salt and sand. Brett pulls on his shirt, dropping his keys. Picking them up he reminds Taylah of the time they hid their dad's thongs in the sand, burying them nearby as a joke. They were never found again and David had to run back to the car, bitumen burning his feet.

Before making their way up to the main strip they both turn back to the water again, looking out. The flagged section is packed full of people. Sand still covered with towels. The blue stretches out forever, making the thousands of bare skinned bodies seem like nothing. All condensed into one tight spot where the water meets the sand. The calm, where Taylah and Brett floated for over an hour out past the break, seems only a few metres away.

Brett nods his head. 'You always feel much further out, hey.'

***

A cheer erupts from a small bar they walk past. A man in whites punches his bat into the air on a TV screen hooked up to the outside wall. Men watching slap each other's backs and drink to the score. Taylah and Brett read the screen before moving on next door to the gelato shop. The sticky smell of waffle cones confirms their choice. They grin. Lining up along the glass with all of the other waiting customers, they point at the thick waves of flavour and weigh up how much they can eat. After five more minutes in the sun behind a family who peel off one by one with cups of rainbow or chocolate while mum stays at the counter to pay, Brett gets a taste of the Ferrero Rocher. Taylah asks to try the blueberry, then the rum and raisin, and settles on coconut rough, a fist-sized scoop balanced on warm crispy cone. Brett goes for a classic: Hokey Pokey. He sucks the top small balls of caramel out of the vanilla. Taylah licks hers around in a circle, moving fast to stop the brown drips. They hang out on the pavement at the front of the bar and give a few minutes to the game.

'Corr,' Brett can't help himself as a catch is missed. 'You've gotta be kidding.'

Taylah smiles at him and swallows the last of her ice cream. Two tables down, a mix of families sing Happy Birthday to a young boy. Sparklers explode off his blue cake, and he grins holding his hands up in front of his eyes, protecting his face from any sparking ash. The burning smell takes Taylah back to New Years, at Steph and Mike's place in the city. It will be another year again before they know it, she thinks. The boy pretends to blow the sparkler out as they all finish singing, before the flame dies. A plate of fish and chips a waitress has just delivered to the people in front of them grabs both Taylah and Brett's attention. They're hungry. The waitress glances up to the TV screen as everyone calls out at the game again, losing herself to the fuss for a second before heading back into the kitchen.

CHAPTER 10

Anyone trying to get inside the already-renowned Lindt chocolate café in the middle of the city, brown brick and gold interior at the top end of a pedestrianised street, around 9:45 am that Monday, would have done what we'd all likely do: frown at the closed electric doors, knowing the café is definitely open and other people are already in there, step back and forward again under the sensor when the doors fail to automatically open, lean forward to peer through the dark glass with one hand up to your brow. See the man. See the gun.

The man, already charged with a long string of sexual assaults and being an accessory to the murder of his ex-wife, started his morning there drinking tea and eating a slice of chocolate cake, sitting for a whole hour in the café, duffel bag at his feet, before changing outfits in the restroom. Before finding the café manager. Having the automatic front doors disabled, locked. So that the day could really begin.

The police are called from the inside. It's a hostage situation, wickedly outside the norm of this hot country with its notoriously strict gun laws. Two decades earlier, a collective loss of life actually spurred regulations which, unlike elsewhere, don't actively exacerbate the existing violence. It's especially irregular as the man has a shotgun and this is happening not out in the bush but here in the busiest city. In other places this might make the news, but probably not in the same way. *This* is not the type of thing that happens *here*. This is Australia. Land of the young and safe and free. As the situation accelerates in severity it's elevated to terrorism of international importance. Some swift alliteration charges the constantly rolling headlines: for seventeen immediate hours, and afterward for weeks and months more, the country is a maelstrom furiously absorbed by the Sydney Siege.

The trains keep running over and underground. Christmas carols continue to play on loop in all the shops. But lunchtime crowds are thicker than at the close of a usual cubicle Monday. Public transport packs with people pushing to get out of the city. Street blocks are quickly cordoned off and media rush to circle the block. Coffee lines are abandoned. Computers are closed down. Heads turn quickly to look back over shoulders at every sound, expecting gunshots or the ripping heat of an explosion. Like we're so used to watching in the movies. By the afternoon the CBD train tunnels don't push much more around than air, concrete flutes singing to no-one across the city. Only the bullet-proofed cops creep in, kept in frame the whole time by the shadowing, texting, nodding, breath-holding, competing-for-the-angles news crews and a few over-interested amateurs, capturing it all in a different way on their various more-mobile devices, themselves suited up in jeans or high school uniforms.

The man with the shotgun – tall, bearded, something other from the outset, pegged as a threat even without the sawn-off shotgun but now directly threatening – claims allegiance to a black Islamic flag that hostages hold up against the chocolate shop windows. Shock circulates. No one can believe what's happening and that it's happening here. This idea is repeated all around the country: surely not here, why here, how here. The usually real and conceptual distance from everywhere else, everywhere North and East and West, where the Troubles are, is suddenly closed. Bordering oceans and time zones momentarily make no difference.

The gunman's face is found in earlier photographs and it catches like wildfire, his frown and open mouth burning under the electric headlines, a one-man manifestation of the Radicalisation Issue long flooding the news. At the time there's nothing but the disabled doors and the flag forcefully pressed to the window for the news crews, white writing on black cloth, a declaration of faith, for hours until the first hostages escape. Afterwards the recounted imagery grips: the man, the headband, large duffle bag and the gun being pulled out, aiming people to the ground – that polished floor thousands tread each week – making the Manager phone the police, the back exit, demands for more flags and news interviews and to speak to the Prime Minister, making hostages make social media videos, humans turned shields, the pick-and-mix mountains of shiny wrapped chocolate by the front door flavoured chocolate orange, strawberries and cream, tropical, champagne, coconut, Spring.

***

The country outside the police no-go zone doesn't stop, but it does slow right down. One of the last days of the school year isn't broken like usual into lesson plans, but counted in minutes between ad breaks on the lunchroom TV and the seconds it takes to refresh a phone's newsfeed. Staff hold off heading back to the classroom longer than the kids do. Taylah's Principal nods with the rest of the teachers in front of the staffroom TV, speechless, in disbelief. Kids' plastic glad wrap and sultana packs are thrown into the bin after a few quick final runs across the oval. Naïve to the gunman holding eighteen people hostage in their city, the children burst for their Christmas cut-and-paste activities to continue, lining up together in two sweating lines outside their closed classrooms.

Caleb's alright and Taylah's alright. Brett's alright. Their friends are fine. Liz and David are alright once they know their city-dwelling kids are far away from the firing line. None of them know anyone inside. Calls ring out across the country, and everyone that's okay, whose loved ones are safe, half-turn themselves back to work until they're graced with home time.

***

Taylah and Caleb run out of words to send to each other, and agree that she'll pick him up after school at the station. Parking illegally, half over a yellow line like the rest of the cars that can't find a park and usually are never here to have to do, she hurries from Facebook to Twitter. People crowd onto the outbound platform, faces down. Phones out. Buzzing. An electric ring. She flicks to what's trending and the story fills her feed without her having to search for anything.

Just shy of six hours in, there are people all around Taylah as she waits outside the station for Caleb's train. Everything seems to stop as she watches online two sprinting escapees make their way out. Empty hands held up high, their terrorised faces collapse behind the barricaded safety of the national police. They all read about it together. Scroll faster. Replay the footage. Hold their breath. A loudspeaker crackle pierces through the silence and the crowd collectively jumps at the announcement of the incoming train. The train eases to a stop and the doors open, carriage loads of city workers pour out and day-tired commuters slouching towards the western suburbs push in. Taylah spies Caleb's head above the crowd as he makes his way out, and punches her hand into the air to wave until he sees her. He swims between people glued to their screens and they collide, arms wrapped tight. The train moves on. Caleb runs his fingers through Taylah's hair.

'What do we do?' he asks.

'Go home I guess,' Taylah sighs. 'Watch the news.'

***

Reports wash out for hours. Some real. Some unreal. The official flow of news is plugged everywhere, but the internet burns with information. Demands are pushed over hostage's personal social media pages. Mainstream media trip over terrorism, religion, welfare. The gunman's identity is tracked and his story speedily unravelled. Questions are asked about state handouts from places high up the ladder. That is one of the first questions to come up, as the facts oscillate for hours between Islamic Death Cult and Lone Mad Man With A Gun: exactly how much government welfare had this man been given? This lone and ill *or* mad and formally-associated terrorist was here, and we supported him, so what does that mean for The Tax-Payer? In suits and in safety this seems a sign that it's much too easy to get onto Easy Street.

People shake their heads to each other, fish-gaped mouths with no words for how close this kind of violence suddenly is. The store that it's happening in is what makes it super-surreal – the chocolate brand we buy Christmas and Easter bunnies and share-boxes from. The exact café worth leaving the shopping mall or Harbour water for, where you pop in for coffee and something sweet, photographing the monstrous chocolate sundaes when holiday trips bring you into the city.

***

They are home and hungry despite it all. Caleb makes rice, checking the amount of water he's put into the rice cooker with Taylah, as always. Taylah reheats yesterday's chicken curry in the microwave, stirring it between hot revolutions just as the bubbles kick in around the Tupperware rim. When the rice is fork fluffed and ready, Caleb spoons it out onto last year's gifted housewarming plates. Taylah adds the curry and Caleb slides fresh greenery from the chopping board on top. Taylah sucks her burnt fingertips as they put their dinner down on the coffee table in front of the TV, her skin pink from not bothering with a tea towel when picking up the hot plastic. Caleb kisses the ends of each of her fingers, fixing them, and they tuck in.

Three more hostages find their way out of a back exit and fire escape. Taylah and Caleb and their neighbours on all five sides, the rest of their hilly low-rise street, the city, this broad country see it happen in real time. The escapees sprinting into the arms of the police, terrified and crying and alive. Their images play on TVs, on computers, laptops, mobile phones as people journey home, and on every kind of screen simultaneously as families gravitate toward each other in their living rooms.

***

Taylah's parents ring while Caleb is already speaking with his, so she takes the call in their bedroom. She sits on the edge of the bed and drops backwards, lying down and letting her feet dangle, speaking first with her mum and then her dad, and afterwards her mum again. They all thank God that they themselves weren't there and share memories of being at that café, drinking those chocolate sundaes. They shake their heads at having some of that chocolate in the fridge and wonder how long it will take for the police to end it. David frowns and gesticulates with his free hand while looking at the TV, the news on a low volume – Taylah knows he is, she can hear it in his voice and see his habits as if she's really there. He flicks through the channels as they speak. He agrees with some of the presenters, repeating the points loud enough for both his wife and daughter to hear, about how certain places and different Gods seem to breed different kinds of things. David near-yells to Taylah down the phone – not at her but to her, out of worry, falling back on the confidence of feeling right in the tone that seems to come with being a dad or maybe just being his kind of man. He tells them there's a need for calling a spade a spade, repeating it more than twice, and says there're differences here and also there's a time and a place for such discussions but Christ right now isn't it. He says the government needs to be more careful with all of this. Connecting some dots easier than others, as we do. Taylah hums back at him in a general way when he pauses mid-thought, not agreeing or disagreeing either, letting him get it out and listening and herself not finding much solid to cling to in the whirling pool of comments and quicksand terror. Her mum, when she's back on again, makes Taylah promise she'll be safe in the city and says to give her love to Caleb too.

***

When their dinner is finished Caleb stacks the plates in the dishwasher and Taylah changes the channel from the news to one showing a film they haven't seen in a good while. An occasional running banner at the bottom of the screen keeps them up to dates with the events as they break. Their neighbour's always-faintly audible TV does too. They spoon on the couch. Knees bent together, phones side by side on the floor, Caleb's arm wrapped over Taylah, loosely holding her stomach. Which she hates. In the ad breaks they slip down through their news feeds, thumbing their blue-white screens in the dark, sweat building through their shirts between Caleb's belly and her back. They come across a viral story, an event that played out on another train line before dusk:

On a packed but eerily quiet train, two women were among rows of commuters who were all watching their phones, being smacked with the news of the crisis. The first woman, a Muslim, wearing a headscarf, reading about the shooter and the Islamic flag, put her phone down and pulled off the material wrapped up around her hair, and got off the train at the next station. The second woman, who had watched the first, breath caught in her chest, hopped off at the next stop too. She followed the first woman and stopped her to say it's okay – that it will be okay. On the platform the two strangers hugged. This is the peak of the short plot. Their clear, quiet, earthquake embrace. The second woman relayed the encounter on her Facebook page, and a third woman read the story and stuck her hand up online, saying "I see you, I'm here too. I'll ride with you." And the embrace bloomed into a story and sprouted a hashtag, #illridewithyou, which moved quicker than the headlines into an organic sort of social media support movement.

Taylah grips onto this. It grips onto her, the story – the sudden appearance, she thinks, of hope. She shares the original post plus any others she finds with the hashtag. She tells Caleb she'll set him up a Twitter account so he can share the hashtag too. He relinquishes his phone and Taylah opens a new browser page, her eye quickly catching those things her boyfriend has recently searched and still has open (phone plan costs, a calendar of upcoming gigs, weekend football results, 18 romantic unique and non-cheesy wedding proposal ideas, the Bureau of Meteorology's storm radar). She sits up quickly with his phone, to 'type better,' and scroll through these romantic unique and non-cheesy ideas with the screen out of Caleb's eyeline. He doesn't notice this, too busy watching the short news update. They replay the early footage again – guns and hostage-held flags. Taylah considers suggestions of skydiving, a scavenger hunt, a knee dropped before *The Kiss* by Rodin in Paris. The imperative of having a hidden photographer or videographer or, ideally, both. She bites her nails and clicks through the rest.

Caleb asks her how it's going and she tells him it's fine. She clicks out of the proposals page and hastily sets up the account, tweeting Caleb's morning train timetable out. They want to tweet out and jump in, knowing the whole narrative of the day could be shaped in a variety of ways. How the story comes together now will change how they actually remember it. And if it's not an us and them game now, they think, it would have been. That's exactly what it would have been. In the coming times, it very well might still be.

'It's so bad isn't it,' Taylah says. 'Terrifying.'

'I know babe,' Caleb says.

'Like, I cannot believe that there is literally a gunman right now holding people hostage in our city. We're here. It's happening right now.' She lies back down in front of Caleb, and turns her head back toward him. 'And what everyone's saying is so bad too. I know they're not on the same level, but like they've already managed to connect Muslims and dole bludgers like some terrorist nut-job is the same issue in just one afternoon.'

'I know what you mean.'

'I wonder what'll happen now.'

'The hashtag thing is good though, isn't it. Heaps of people posting shit.'

'Yeah, so good. Literally everyone on my feed is doing it.'

'Even though probably they never even take public transport,' Caleb adds. 'You going to write about this?' he asks, still scrolling through his phone. 'In your journal thing, I mean. Now you're doing it more again.'

'Mmm,' Taylah thinks, turning her head back to her phone. 'Yeah I guess I should. Like, we're not there but it is here, you know.'

'I can't believe you're still writing it. Nearly a whole year, babe. It's great.'

'I know right. It's the first New Year's resolution I've ever kept.'

'Mmm, you're so resolved now, what a woman,' he jokes.

Taylah laughs. 'It's nice to look back on all the stuff we've done and like how I felt about it.' She pauses, looking ahead at the TV screen. 'All the shit I worry about seems much smaller when you have it all there and can go back to it after what you thought was a huge issue just passes.'

'Yeah.'

'It's been good for Sam though, and all the stuff with Brett. You know, processing rather than going over and over everything all the time. I do that a bit.'

'I know.'

'And it helps you figure out like what you actually think, I think. Like with stuff like this,' Taylah points her phone to the TV. Ads are on, but Caleb catches that she means the hostage crisis. 'Maybe you should try it, next year. That can be your resolution.'

Caleb momentarily considers it. 'I don't have anything to write down though babe. No worries with me, see.' He kisses Taylah's hand and changes the TV channel, flicking between the major stations until the movie comes back on. 'Do you reckon you'll keep doing it next year?'

'Dunno. Maybe.'

***

They drift off just before midnight, carrying themselves to bed when the still air and the narrowness of the lounge seat, the lack of pillows, gets too much. And they sleep through the rest of it. Nearly all of us do. The real early morning unfolds with a pumping shotgun and blood while even the birds sleep. After sixteen hours the end comes. A bang. A few breaths. The assault team shoots in. Glass breaks. Paramedics wait. The brown layers of the corner lot are given a once-over, a cop gives the okay from the top of the building, shining a flashlight towards the others in the dark, working to breathe steady, getting paid overtime, ready to flood in. They move and then it's the end. Three dead. The gunman. The store manager. A customer. Paramedics move up and down the pedestrian street, frozen in time as their photographs are captured by the ready cameras – iconic images of hostages alive, police with exhausted eyes, the green and red crossing man alternating on the streetlights behind them.

It's over and it's not over. Some part of it keeps hanging in the air. In the morning, between picking a necklace and brushing her teeth, Taylah decides to take the train to work even though it means going the long way. She and Caleb lock the front door and leave together, riding down four flights in the dinging old elevator with another couple of bleary-eyed residents. Runners pass them on the sidewalk. A pelaton of cyclists pulls up at the lights. At the station there's a tense calm in the morning crowd. Strangers swap half-smiles, unsure what to make of everything they seemed to share last night. She and Caleb hold hands on the platform, yawning in the morning sun. They send their route out again into cyberspace, adding the viral tag, meaning it. Caleb's train comes first. They kiss and keep their fingers linked until the distance is too much, then he follows the rest of the platform on and jumps between the doors before they slide shut. A train controller riding the carriage at the back nods at Taylah as the train takes off past her. She takes the stairs and crosses to her northbound platform. There are only two stops she needs to take but she tweets the route out again, identifying herself. Blonde hair, white shirt, blue pants.

At the site of the scene, where new safety barriers have been put up for the flocking crowds that fully surround the closed chocolate shop, people bring bouquets of flowers. Taylah texts Caleb a link to a story with lots of photos. City workers come in before work, come down on their lunch breaks from their towering offices, stay back after their workdays have finished. High school kids detour there before getting the bus. Tourists trek in from the Harbour following their paper and electronic maps, even more than typically would. Young couples meet there after work shifts. Parents brings their kids in all weekend. Thousands of plastic-wrapped bunches takeover the pedestrian strip. Chrysanthemums, carnations, gerberas, orchids, roses, lilies. It's red and yellow, purple, orange, pink, white, and green. A full garden of floral tributes. A harvest. A rainbow sea of flowers.

The gunman isn't claimed by known terrorist links and he is reduced to a loner, unstable, mentally unfit. The terror of the actual event isn't any less but the way it's seen, the way it's handled and carefully spoken around, shifts.

The store manager who was killed is elevated as more and more of a hero as the aftermath drags on – for what happened inside, for who he was before to everyone who he worked with and who knew him. His parents and family and male partner of fourteen years, unable to ever wed, speak in short news clips cut between images of the makeshift memorial outside the store. The customer who died as well – a lawyer, blonde, white, beautiful – as the police stormed in to end everything, is mourned there too among the flowers. She's tied to her husband and children, now motherless. The picture of loss is complete.

The vast web of people and problems is illuminated as each new and infinite connection becomes clear. Ideas of money and men and violence and full health and what kinds of things happen where, what things happen to who. The image of religion. How we find out about and capture and share moments in our shared lives, the good and the bad and mundane and memorial. What unexpected punctuations mean for making a community.

Over a week after the siege end, in the bright sunlight of the afternoon, blue sky as usual with birds and occasional planes passing overhead, Martin Place heaves with people coming to leave flowers and see the flowers. News crews hold their territory. Politicians rotate through. People record it all and each other. Amongst the day, a car pulls up at the end of the street. A couple emerge, he in a sharp black suit with a white rose pinned to his chest and she head to toe in white, lips done and dark hair wrapped, adorned and veiled. They walk up the street with their photographer and wedding party. It's a sight that parts the crowd. She is a vision. The couple pay tribute with all the others, and the Bride bends down amongst the sea of flowers to leave her wedding bouquet. People standing in the place applaud collectively, compelled by the intensity as cameras capture the moment and there's a flash of hope, a movement towards something different and new. Headlines about the Muslim bride and calls for unity spin out internationally. Taylah and Caleb see the viral pictures and decide to go tomorrow. The space keeps becoming, bringing in more flowers and holding bricks, blood, trauma, sirens, news crews, children, strangers, bodies, chocolates, and trains.

ABOUT THE AUTHOR

Ash Watson, PhD, is a writer and sociologist. She grew up in different places along the east coast of Australia and now lives with her wife in Sydney. She studied creative writing and literature before gaining her PhD in Sociology in 2018. Ash is a university-based researcher passionate about how creative methods can help us understand contemporary social issues and our shared visions of the future. She is the creator and editor of *So Fi Zine*, an indie publication for social science and arts cross-disciplinary inquiry, publishing short stories, cartoons, photo essays, poetry and other creative works. She is currently working on her second novel.

Printed in the United States
By Bookmasters